LOVE ON THE RUN

Discard

***Other Five Star Titles
by Shari MacDonald:***

Stardust

LOVE ON THE RUN

SHARI MacDONALD

Five Star
Unity, Maine

Five Star Christian Fiction Series.

Published in conjunction with WaterBrook Press, a division of Random House, Inc.

Library of Congress Cataloging-in-Publication Data

MacDonald, Shari.
    Love on the run / Shari MacDonald.
      p. cm.
    ISBN 0-7862-2708-7 (hc : alk. paper)
    1. Women in the advertising industry — Fiction.
  2. Elopement — Fiction. 3. Sisters — Fiction. I. Title.
    PS3563.A2887 L6 2000
    813′.54—dc21
                                  00-034720

To my bridesmaids: Kim, Sarah, Susan, Lindy,
and Claire

You've been with me through the tough times (as
if I had to remind you!), and you were by my side
on the most joyful day of my life. Thank you for all your
help and offers of help, for listening to endless wedding
details, for letting me cry when "planning stress"
overwhelmed me, for throwing and attending the best
showers ever given, for packing my honeymoon
bags at the last minute (a neat trick, since we didn't know
where I was going), for bonding with each other in a way
I never thought possible, for staying up with me
half the night before my wedding day, for asking me
(a thousand times), "Have you eaten?" and most of all,
for sharing in my excitement, hysteria, and happiness.

I pray I will always live in the circle of your love.

ONE

From the moment she stepped into the sleek, bullet-shaped elevator that serviced her upscale office building, Catherine Salinger felt a strange, sinking feeling in the pit of her stomach—not a good sign at all, considering the fact that she was heading *up* to the eighth floor.

Had she been inclined to believe in such things, she might have said that something was in the air or that the feeling was a sort of premonition. But being a dependable, rational sort, she dismissed the feeling as latent indigestion caused by the previous night's meal, made a mental note to eschew all restaurants serving steaks rare enough to moo, and set her mind to spending the next twelve hours doing what she did best: running the Salinger & Associates advertising agency like a well-oiled machine.

The elevator doors opened with a friendly hum, and Catherine stepped confidently into the agency's opulent lobby. White-bleached walls gleamed beneath warm summer sunlight streaming through the windows, giving the entire foyer a cheerful glow. Behind the gray-and-white marble receptionist's desk sat a virile-looking man with high cheekbones and a mischievous glint in his eye.

Catherine smiled in spite of herself. True, it still bothered her a bit that Billy Guzman's face was the first she saw each morning. Although she headed a cutting-edge advertising agency, Catherine's personal tastes ran to the classic and the conventional—and there was certainly *nothing* conventional about her twenty-four-year-old male receptionist. It was taking her some time to adjust to the fact that she now had a man taking messages for her: particularly one who worked part-time in the mornings simply so he could spend the rest of the day pursuing his dream of becoming—Catherine shuddered at the thought—an actor.

Only in L.A., she thought wryly.

"GOOD morning, Ms. Salinger!" the young man said with what Catherine took to be caffeine-induced enthusiasm. With one hand he thrust at her a short stack of pink message slips; with the other, he reached up to adjust the tiny telephone headset that perched ridiculously atop his dark, closely cropped hair, its mouthpiece extending down his masculine jaw line. He was impeccably dressed in a fashionable red tie and crisp white shirt that stylishly covered his model's physique.

Catherine gave him a look of measured approval. She took no issue with his personal appearance; Billy made a good first impression with clients. Neither was she concerned with his social skills; he had a wonderful telephone persona, though he did tend to answer occasionally as Jimmy Durante or John Wayne. There was no question, in fact, that Billy was a generally able receptionist. Unfortunately, he was also a . . . er, quirky one.

More than once, for example, he had attempted to use his position at the ad agency to finagle impromptu auditions with major advertisers. Last week after hearing that representatives from the National Fruit Council would be visiting, he'd shown up for work in a giant banana costume. A month earlier, he'd pulled out a Mr. Microphone, jumped up on the receptionist's desk, and crooned "You Light Up My Life" to the astonished president of a local electric company.

Catherine couldn't forget that day if she tried.

And she certainly *had* tried.

All in all, she would have preferred that the company have a nice, quiet female receptionist. But she wasn't about to fire Billy now. She couldn't, wouldn't, discriminate against him because of his gender. Besides, she liked Billy in spite of his quirks and, if pressed, would admit she even felt a bit sentimental about him.

Hiring Billy had been among the last of many questionable management decisions Catherine's father had made as company president. Days later, Edward Salinger had collapsed from a heart attack during a major presentation. Three hours later, he was dead.

That had been just two months ago, and the eight weeks since then had been among the most difficult periods of her life—equal in their own way to the loss of her mother many years before. For in the days following her father's death Catherine had been faced not only with a great personal tragedy, but with the prospect of taking over leadership of the agency her father had built into one of the strongest in the city.

She was the perfect choice, having been her father's second-in-command for several years. But friends and family had warned her she might be biting off more than she could chew. "You need time to grieve," they told her. "It's too much to expect of yourself."

Catherine ignored such warnings. She had always set high standards—for herself and for those around her. She saw no reason to lower them now. Besides, she was handling the loss of her father just fine—or at least, as well as could be expected. The week he died, she had taken several days off—an unprecedented event in the history of her employment at Salinger & Associates—in order to plan the funeral. Since then she had, according to the advice in several books on grieving, scheduled into her overfilled day-planner time to visit his grave, to sit and think about him, to cry.

Some people said it was cold of her—*inhuman,* even—to cope so matter-of-factly; she'd heard the murmurings around the office. But whether *they* liked it or not, that was how Catherine handled pain: She *dealt* with it, the same way she did every other problem that needed to be faced. That's what made her a great executive. She had suffered a great loss, but that loss was personal and business was, as the saying goes, business.

"Good morning, Billy." She graciously inclined her head, returning the greeting.

"Robin was looking for you just a little while ago," he said. "At least, she asked me if I'd seen you. She sounded a bit . . . uh, panicked."

Catherine frowned. It wasn't like her assistant to get her feathers ruffled. The ad agency was filled with high-strung executive types and quirky, barely reliable creative geniuses—Billy wasn't the only unstable lunatic running around. But Catherine could always count on efficient Robin to coolly dispatch her orders and maintain some degree of control in the office. Now that she thought about it, though, Robin *had* been acting a bit strangely in recent weeks—uncharacteristically losing things, and at times even snapping at Catherine.

"It's probably stress about the baby," she said reasonably, deciding to extend a bit of grace. "She's due to deliver in . . ." Catherine pulled her jumbo-sized, leather-bound day-planner out from under her arm and opened it to a page flagged by a thick, laminated marker. In less than two seconds, her gaze landed upon the date she had written in red, circled in purple, and highlighted in green. "Three weeks and six days."

Billy arched an eyebrow. "I'm impressed."

"What? That she's still working?" Catherine's brow furrowed. Was that a criticism of her workaholic tendencies? Robin was, after all, *her* assistant.

"Yeah. I mean, I think it's great and all. But *WOW*. I don't know if I could do it." Catherine relaxed in the face of his obvious enthusiasm. Of course Billy wouldn't question her. No one at the office would, except possibly Robin herself, if she was pushed to it and her hormones were on overdrive—which these days they *always* were. And, of course, Daphne—but sisters didn't count.

"You couldn't do it. That's why you're a man."

Billy laughed. "You raving feminist."

"That's *Ms.* Raving Feminist to you. And you'd better watch it, bub, or I'll have you beheaded. You know I can do it."

"Beggin' yer pardon, ma'am," he responded with a bad Cockney accent. "I never meant no 'arm . . ."

Catherine ignored him. Her eyes flickered back to the enormous planner, open in her hands. "Robin won't be around much longer though. Her maternity leave starts in just over a week. She's supposed to start training her replacement . . ." Her slender index finger traced down a list of notes written under the alphabetized section heading: ROBIN. "Yes, there it is. Today." Her heart sank a bit. She depended upon her able assistant more than she cared to admit and drew little comfort from the knowledge that Robin planned to come back to work part-time in the fall.

Oh, well. Catherine purposely banished the troublesome thought from her mind. It didn't matter. At least, it didn't have to. Robin was a fantastic assistant and as good a friend as an employee could be, but she'd be the second, right after Catherine, to admit she wasn't perfect. Certainly the employment agency would send someone equally capable to fill her place. And if not—well, Catherine thought with confidence, she would just train the replacement herself.

"A woman named Carol Kincaid came in earlier," Billy offered, "saying she was here to see Robin. That may have been the temp."

"Perfect." Catherine snapped the book shut and tucked back a tendril of blond hair that had worked its way out of her tight chignon. A downward glance and a one-handed pat confirmed that everything else—from the top of her carefully coiffed, honey-colored hair to the tips of her black crocodile Stuart Weitzman pumps—was in order. "Things are working out according to plan." Her smile was butter smooth. "Just the way I like it."

"Yes, General Patton," he agreed amicably. Catherine saluted and turned away as the telephone began to ring. "Good morning. Salinger & Associates. How may I direct your call?" As she headed into the main office, the sound of Billy's rich, theater-trained voice was drowned out by the dull roar of whirring copy machines, piped-in Muzak, and ongoing verbal battles between various members of the creative staff.

"Good morning, Gary. Saundra. Dave." Catherine nodded amiably at each employee as she approached. "Morning, Teri. How's the Happy Dwarf Cookie account coming? I want an update on the little monsters by three o'clock." And: "Steve! I heard about your meeting with the All-You-Can-Eat-Meat smorgasbord guys . . . No, I didn't know you were a vegetarian . . . He insisted you try a *what?* Well, I'm just glad no one got seriously hurt."

With quick, efficient steps she made her way down the narrow hallway that led to her assistant's office, located directly outside her own. As she passed, copywriters, graphic designers, account execs, and creative directors worked intently at their desks on either side of her path—some quietly brainstorming, composing, or designing; others arguing loudly.

"I'm telling you, 'Hot Stuff' is the hook we're looking for," a male voice proclaimed from behind the partition Catherine was passing.

"But it's a secondhand store," a woman protested. "It doesn't make sense."

"That's the *point*," the man said acidly. "Nobody thinks of things in resale shops as being 'hot.' We can change the company's whole image."

Catherine stopped and peered over the top of the cubicle to find two of her youngest and newest copywriters glaring at one another.

"Tracy. Sam," she said with an exaggerated smile. "I'd just like to take a moment to thank you personally for sharing your strategy with the entire office. It's so refreshing to start the day out with a good screaming match. Sets a nice tone for the entire day. Really." The pair responded with guilty looks.

"Uh . . . sorry, Catherine."

"I assume this is about the St. Francis account?" One month earlier, representatives from the St. Francis charity group—owners of one of the largest 'chains' of secondhand stores in the country—had approached Catherine and asked if Salinger & Associates could help reinvent their image. Because of the charity's work with the homeless, Catherine had agreed to take on the assignment *pro bono*.

"Ye-es," Tracy stammered. "We're working on the campaign."

"I think we should go with 'Hot Stuff'," Sam insisted. "We can use the copy to talk about how people want to look like 'hot stuff,' so they buy name-brand merchandise. But, really, the stuff at St. Frank can be every bit as 'hot.' " He arched his eyebrows for emphasis. "Get it?"

"I get it, I get it," Catherine said.

Sam gave Tracy a cocky grin.

"However," Catherine continued, "it's important to remember that we *are* talking about a secondhand store, here. And there's more than one way merchandise can be, er . . . 'hot.' "

Sam blinked at Catherine. "What? You mean . . . stolen?" His joyful expression collapsed, one facial muscle at a time, as understanding dawned upon him.

"Would *you* want to buy a 'hot' stereo from a secondhand shop?"

The copywriter's face flushed an unattractive, blotchy pink. Tracy beamed.

"Nice try, tiger," Catherine told Sam, using her most soothing tone. "But I wouldn't set up the storyboards just yet. Keep trying. You'll get it."

As she walked away, she could still hear Tracy chortling. Catherine couldn't blame her. Her intention hadn't been to embarrass Sam, but the man did have a tendency to get a little uppity. She hadn't been able to resist the urge to take him down just a peg.

Catherine strode purposefully into Robin's well-organized, tastefully decorated office and scanned the room. At the center was the solid pine desk from which Robin ran "command central." A rich, cobalt-blue velvet couch stretched out along the nearest wall, and every bit of available wall space was taken up with the black-framed stills from popular TV commercials and blowups of award-winning print ads that served as testament to the agency's success.

Her eyes barely registered these familiar details, tracking instead on the two figures in the far corner. The closest one—a matronly woman Catherine guessed to be in her late forties—stood looking around curiously. Thick, wiry, salt-and-pepper-colored hair was piled high on her head in a modified beehive. Her blouse was plain, Catherine noticed, but neat, and its cream color complemented perfectly the navy blue slacks that were hiked up a bit too high at her generous middle. As the woman turned to her companion, her sensible, thick-soled shoes made slight imprints in the thick carpet beneath her feet.

Catherine's eyes drifted from this curious stranger to the other, more familiar figure, shod in sensible shoes of her own and wearing a sunny yellow jumper that made Catherine want to squint. Though it was still early morning, the young woman looked ready to call it a day. Catherine watched as her very pregnant assistant shifted her considerable weight from one foot to another, standing now with her right arm bent, hand propped against her back for support, and her left arm extended in front of her as she pointed to the cabinets that held thousands of file records related to the company's accounts.

Catherine's lips twitched. "Good morning, Little Teapot."

Robin turned and scrunched her pretty face into a scowl. "I suppose that's a reference to my being 'short and stout'?" At five foot two, she qualified for the first category, but pregnancy had actually left her more 'rotund' than 'stout.'

"Such temper, Mama Maitland! It was simply a reference to the way you were standing. I was admiring your handle and spout." Catherine carefully placed her day-planner and purse on the desk and placed her arms to imitate Robin's.

"Fine," Robin grumbled and began to waddle over to where Catherine stood. "Just don't tip me over."

Catherine settled both hands on her graceful hips.

15

"Please. Tip you over? How would we ever get you back up?"

Robin sniffed. "Cat, this is Carol Kincaid, the temp the employment agency sent over." She turned and indicated the woman who had come to stand beside her. "Carol, this is your new boss." She clutched Carol's arm and muttered in whispered *sotto voce,* "You poor soul." The woman looked at Robin uncertainly.

Catherine smiled serenely and reached out to clasp her hand. "Hello, Carol. I'm Catherine."

This seemed to relax her, and the woman smiled timidly. "How do you do, dear?"

Her tone was alarmingly motherish. Catherine tensed up immediately, yet managed to keep a stiff smile on her face. She was thirty-one years old, long past the age when she allowed herself to be addressed like a child. *But,* she carefully reminded herself, *Carol doesn't know me yet. Once she does, she'll treat me with the same respect everyone else does—I'll see to that.* And if she didn't—well, "Mrs. Fields" would be out the door before the woman could say 'milk-and-cookies.' Catherine was determined to keep things firmly under control in the office. Billy Guzman was simply an aberration, as was Robin. And Daphne. And . . .

Robin cleared her throat, bringing Catherine back to the present. "I'm so pleased to meet you, Carol," Catherine said in a cool, measured voice. "Don't let Robin scare you. Those are the hormones talking. I assure you, life at Salinger & Associates is an employee's dream."

"Maybe employees who previously worked for Stalin," Robin said, lumbering over to her desk chair.

Catherine threw her a sidelong glance. "You'll find that I don't expect my employees to stay later than I do. . . ."

"Seven-thirty P.M. . . . *when* you're lucky."

"And our salaries are quite competitive. . . ."

16

"Hazard pay," Robin puffed. She pushed several long, blond corkscrew curls out of her face and lowered herself awkwardly into her chair.

"Robin, what's that supposed to mean?"

She shrugged. "Admit it, Cat. You're an . . . uh, *interesting* boss to work for."

" '*Interesting.*' " Robin certainly was a firecracker these days. Catherine folded her arms across her chest. *What is in those prenatal vitamins she's taking, anyway?* "And how, exactly, am I . . . 'interesting'?"

"Oh . . . ," Robin hedged. "*You* know."

"Actually, as it so happens, I *don't* know. *Enlighten me.*" Catherine's expression froze in a stiff, toothy smile. A little teasing was one thing; an obvious challenge to her authority was another.

"Well . . ." Robin glanced up and caught Catherine's glare. She hesitated. "Well . . . for example, the way you keep extra pantyhose at work."

"Lots of women do that."

"Perhaps. But sorted in different file folders according to sheerness, color, *and* manufacturer?"

Catherine shook her head. "I don't see what's so interesting about that."

"Okay, then." Robin tried to lean forward in her seat for emphasis, found that she couldn't because of her enormous belly, and settled back with an exasperated sigh. "How's this? Tell Carol how you file your own papers before I can get to them, then throw a conniption fit when I can't find anything?"

"You know how I think," Catherine said calmly. "You always figure it out eventually."

"And then, there's that, that . . . thing." Robin waggled a puffy finger at Catherine's bulging day-planner, which

17

now sat several inches from her computer monitor. "Your Day Gladiator."

"It's a Time Champion," Catherine said wearily. "And you know I'd be lost without it."

"Is that the new time-management system that's out? I hear it's really good," Carol Kincaid's perky voice cut into the conversation. Both Catherine and Robin looked at her in surprise, having nearly forgotten she was even in the room.

"It *is* really good," Catherine said firmly.

"If you use it properly," Robin agreed. "But," she turned to Carol, "Catherine's obsessed. She's like . . . a Time Warrior *junkie*."

"Time *Champion*." The look Catherine gave her was cool. "And I am not a junkie. I'm *not* obsessed."

"Oh, yeah?" Robin snatched the leather binder off the desk before Catherine could make a move to stop her. "Let's look at today's list: 'Six-fifteen: Wake up,' " Robin read out loud. " 'Six-sixteen to six-twenty-seven: Get ready for workout. Six-twenty-eight to six-thirty-six: Drive to gym. Six-thirty-seven to seven-twenty-five: Weights and cardio. Seven-twenty-six to seven-fifty-five: Get ready for work.' " She looked up, horrified. "For goodness' sake, Catherine, who plans stuff at six-*sixteen* or six-*thirty-two*? You don't call that obsessed? Oh, and get this: Just before 'Eight-twenty: start working,' you've got: 'Eight-ten to eight-nineteen: Free time.' Free time? What can you do with nine minutes of 'free time'?"

Catherine reached across the desk and snatched her planner out of Robin's grasp. "Nothing, now," she said dryly. "Maybe I should scribble in 'Fire Robin.' "

Robin turned to Carol. "Even when Cat doesn't have something planned ahead of time," she whispered in a conspiratorial voice, "she'll go back and write it into her book after the fact."

Catherine refused to get drawn into an argument. "I like knowing where I've been and what I've done as well as where and when I'm going." Carol continued to stare at her with an expression that conveyed a mixture of horror and motherly concern. "It keeps things clear in my mind. I had no idea it offended you so deeply."

"It doesn't offend me." Robin ventured a weak smile. "I'm sorry I got after you like that."

"Hormones. I'm telling you, it's hormones. *Please* have this baby already, and put the rest of us out of our misery." Catherine folded her arms resolutely across her chest.

"I wasn't criticizing you," Robin insisted. "All I said was, you're *interesting*. You know very well that you don't ask for the same things normal bosses do."

"What, like getting me a latté every morning? If that's all I wanted, I could have replaced you years ago with a Mr. Coffee. Just as effective, without all the back talk."

"Did I hear someone say 'coffee'?" a smooth male voice broke in.

Catherine turned and found herself face-to-face with a slim, professional-looking man in his early thirties. His hair was light, nearly white-blond, and had been cut into a boyish style: short on the sides, floppy on top. The suit he wore was obviously expensive, fitted impeccably, but rendered a touch offbeat by the band-collar shirt and suspenders.

Catherine tried to keep her expression stern, but the newcomer's smile was warm and infectious. As her eyes met his, he grinned widely.

"My dear Catherine."

"Hello, Davis." She greeted her advertising director with a friendly nod. Davis Pierce was brilliant at managing and coordinating all aspects of the advertising business. If only he would abandon his irritating habit of asking her out on dates.

Months ago, she was sure, he had realized and accepted that Catherine was not interested. But he kept on asking, presumably because he loved the thrill of the chase.

"What do you say, Cat? We've never been out to coffee together," he said, sounding hopeful.

"Davis, we've never been out *anywhere* together," she said.

"My point exactly," he replied brightly.

"And there's a *reason* for that."

"Oh." Davis folded his arms against his well-tailored chest and considered this for a moment. "I hope for your sake it's a good one?"

"It's a *great* one."

"What a shame."

Catherine kept her facial muscles drawn into a serious expression. "As a matter of fact, I have *many* good reasons, not the least of which is: I adore you, but you're not my type. We've been over this before," she reminded him. *"Daily."*

Carol Kincaid was staring from Catherine to Davis, then back to Robin.

"Don't worry," Robin gently assured her. "It's a ritual between these two. Every day for the past year or so, Davis comes in and asks Catherine out. And every day she says no. It's harmless. Nobody's lost their job over it."

"Yet," Catherine grumbled.

"Come on, Catherine." Davis batted his eyelashes in what was, apparently, supposed to be a winning fashion. The result, however, simply made him look ridiculous. "Say yes."

"No."

" *'Yes,'* " he insisted.

"No."

"No."

"Ha-ha. Nice try." Catherine's eyes danced. She really

20

didn't care to date Davis. But she couldn't help but enjoy their verbal jousting.

"But you haven't been out on a date in for*ever.*"

"Please. Stop with the flattery . . . you're embarrassing me." Catherine spoke in an exaggerated monotone that belied her words. "You sweet-talker, you."

"I'm serious. A gorgeous, intelligent woman like you should be the toast of the town," Davis insisted.

"And instead, I'm just burnt toast?"

"Oohhhh, Cat." Davis was the picture of sympathy. "Don't think of yourself that way. I don't." He draped one arm around her shoulder and gave her a look of great pity.

Catherine finally laughed. "All right, Davis. That's enough. Paws off the merchandise." With one hand, she firmly grasped his wrist and removed it from her person. "I may be your friend, but I'm also your boss. And that's the end of the story. It's time to get back to work."

Davis glanced down at the arm that now hung loosely at his side. "This has got to be some kind of sexual harassment," he said glumly.

"Sexual harassment applies only to work-related issues."

"Perfect!" He perked up at that. "I *am* at work."

"You know what I mean." Catherine would not be moved. "It was a good effort, but your argument leaves a lot to be desired."

"I know, I know. I'll get back to you when I have my angle perfected."

"You do that," she said generously.

"In the meantime," he said, adopting a more businesslike tone, "why don't we touch base once more about next week's Apollo Athletics presentation?"

Catherine met his eyes and smiled again. At last, Davis was discussing a subject she was comfortable with. For the past month, her greatest passion had been working on the agency's upcoming bid to represent the hot-shot shoe company *Business World* had named "Fastest Growing Corporation of the Year."

She flipped through the pages of her day-planner. "You and I are meeting with Daphne and the creative team at two o'clock to talk about it."

"Two o'clock?" Robin asked innocently. "Not two-thirteen or two-twenty-six?"

Catherine consulted her book. "Unless, Davis, you want to meet one-on-one first? In that case, I can squeeze you in at ten-seventeen, right between 'Pluck Eyebrows' and 'Torture Robin.' "

"I'll take it." Davis grabbed a felt-tip pen from Robin's desk and scribbled the time on his palm in black ink.

Catherine cringed at his sloppy organization and had to look away. "Speaking of people I need to punish: Has anyone seen Daphne? She was supposed to drop off some files at my house last night, and she never showed up. I'm thinking thumbscrews or water torture."

Davis shrugged. "She wasn't in her office when I went by."

"I heard someone mention she called in to say she'd be late," Robin offered. "Something about her car."

Catherine wasn't surprised. Though her younger sister could afford a brand-new vehicle, she insisted on keeping "Smiley," the battered, wheezing junker she'd driven since high school, stubbornly citing "mother-Pacer bonding."

"Car trouble? Daphne? There's a shocker," Catherine grumbled. She walked over to the credenza and reached into a wire basket to pull out the mail Robin had sorted for her. "All right. Well, when you see her, tell her I'm looking for her."

"Will do," Davis promised. He leaned back against the doorjamb, clearly in no hurry to go. Catherine knew he wouldn't get back to work until she did.

She flipped through the stack of envelopes and magazines in her hand. "Robin? Isn't the *Ad Update* supposed to come this week? There's going to be a feature on all the bids for the Apollo Athletics ad contract. Remember, they called to interview me about it awhile back? I want to see how the article turned out."

"I have *no* idea where it is," Robin said a bit too quickly. "None at all. But I'll let you know as soon as it comes in." She waved both hands in the air, as if "shooing" Catherine into her office. "You're too busy to worry about details like that. Why don't you just go ahead and get to whatever you were going to—"

"Is this what you're looking for?" On the other side of the room, Carol Kincaid held up an innocuous-looking newspaper, folded in thirds.

"Well . . . yes. That's it." Catherine looked at her in surprise. Thank goodness, the woman was going to work out just fine. "Where on earth did you find it?"

"Robin put it under here just before you came in," Carol said, pointing to a stack of papers marked "To Be Shredded."

Catherine cocked one eyebrow at her assistant.

"That's not really the *Ad Update*," Robin protested. "It . . . uh . . . just looks like it. Let me just take that—" She tried to stand and reach for the paper but in her condition could not move as quickly as Catherine, who was across the room in seconds.

"Let me see that." She swiftly plucked the paper out of Carol's hands. Defeated, Robin threw an imploring look in Davis's direction while Catherine scanned the cover. "Why, look at this," she said with exaggerated enthusiasm. "It *is* the

23

Ad Update! It's a miracle!" Her smile faded, and she fixed Robin with a pointed stare. "All right, missy. What was that all about? Why wouldn't you want me to see—"

"This old rag?" Davis stepped forward and snatched the *Update* away. "Who'd want to read this garbage, anyway? It's like the *National Interrogator* of the ad world." With a deft toss, he threw the prize to Robin, who clutched it to her bosom.

"Davis! You traitor." Catherine narrowed her eyes at him and moved toward Robin's desk.

"Stop!" Robin cried, holding the paper across her chest like a shield. "You wouldn't hit a pregnant woman, would you? I'm a mother, you know. Please don't make my baby an orphan."

"Cut the Shakespeare," Catherine said crisply, holding out one hand, "and give me the paper."

"All right." Robin's shoulders slumped, and the posture made her entire body, and not just her belly, look rounded. "But there's something you should know first."

"Robin . . ." Catherine's voice held a warning.

The woman took a quick visual survey of her surroundings.

"Don't even *think* about running, Speedy Gonzales."

"But, Cat—" she protested.

"Paper, Robin."

"I just—"

"Paper. *Now.*"

Wearing the expression of one who had been sentenced to death, Robin reluctantly allowed the pages to be pulled from her viselike grip.

"For goodness' sake, Robin. It's not as bad as all that, is it? I suppose I've been misquoted or something. If so, I'll get a retraction. Don't worry, I can handle whatever is in here."

"Famous last words." Catherine's assistant looked as if she were going to be sick.

"Don't be silly," Catherine grumbled, her frustration beginning to show. She tucked the paper under her arm, grabbed her Time Champion, mail, and purse, and headed into her office. "Why are you just standing around?" she threw over her shoulder. "Don't the three of you have work to do?"

She grimaced as she went through the door, hating the sound of her voice as it shrilled in her ears. Catherine was typically a tough taskmaster, but rarely did she come across as shrewish—and she certainly didn't want to. It seemed Robin's testiness was starting to affect her, too. She couldn't wait until it was time for the baby to arrive—for her own sake as much as for her assistant's.

Catherine stepped into her office and closed the door firmly behind her. Pausing for just a moment, she closed her eyes and drank in the silence. *There.* She sighed deeply. *Much better.* The company might be filled with dancing bananas, dueling writers, and hysterical pregnant women, but at least in her office—the office that had once been her father's—she could find a bit of peace.

It wasn't a sense of her father's presence that calmed her, though she could still smell the traces of his sweet pipe tobacco trapped in the carpet, and his vast library of books still lined the shelves. No, Edward Salinger had been as undisciplined as the rest of the staff and had driven his daughter just as crazy. Though a creative genius, he had never been an astute businessman. Catherine had spent the better part of her professional life trying to put, and then keep, his company in order.

She crossed the executive-style office and settled herself at the antique oak desk that had also been her father's. As was her habit each morning, she flipped open her Time Champion to that day's tasks and consulted her list. "Eight-twenty-one to eight-forty-five: Catch up on correspondence and general reading." She scowled at her watch. Thanks to Robin, she was already six minutes behind schedule.

She reached for her mail, ignoring a stack of envelopes Robin had stamped URGENT and zeroing in on the *Ad Update*. Obviously, Robin thought Cat had been misrepresented in the article; she might as well read what it said and, if necessary, call and confront the editor.

Catherine leaned back in her black leather desk chair, her eyes flickering over the text as she speed-read the front-page feature. Most of the information was old news to her; the article reported that the Apollo Athletics running-shoe company had terminated its relationship with a New York ad group and were accepting pitches from agencies based in Los Angeles, where their company was located. Catherine was quoted as saying that Apollo's search was "an incredible opportunity" for the local companies and that she was confident the shoe company would be impressed by the creativity and professionalism demonstrated by West Coast agencies.

Nothing wrong with that. Catherine considered calling Robin into her office and demanding an explanation for her ridiculous outburst.

And then she saw it.

As she scanned the list of advertising agencies that would be participating in the bidding process, her eyes were drawn to a name that still had the power to cause her great uneasiness.

The Riley Agency. Owned and operated by her father's former partner, Miles Riley. And, if Cat was not mistaken, Miles's elder son, Jonas.

Not that she cared a fig about Jonas. What he did these

days was no concern of hers. Their relationship was over. Finished. *Finito*. End of story.

Hungrily, she devoured the remaining text.

The article gave a two-sentence history of the agency, reporting that, after helping found Salinger & Riley, a major force in the advertising business throughout the early eighties, Miles Riley had started up his own company in San Francisco late in the fall of 1986. Although a satellite office had been maintained in Los Angeles, Riley's main office— and primary sphere of influence—had stayed in the Bay area.

Until now.

Catherine bit down so hard on her lip that she drew blood. It seemed that on the eve of the potentially lucrative Apollo bid, the Riley Agency had planned a fortuitous move of their main office to the Los Angeles area—and would be bidding for the Apollo account.

She licked away the saltiness and swallowed hard. Miles Riley was back in town. Even more appalling, so was his willfully stubborn, irritatingly self-righteous—and, according to the photo in the paper, still maddeningly gorgeous—older son.

Cat dropped the newsprint on the desk and lowered her head heavily into her hands. No wonder Robin had seized the *Update*; she'd worked at the agency for years and knew of its roots, as well as Catherine's animosity toward the Rileys. Clearly, she thought the news was more than Cat could handle.

Well, I'll show Robin. I'll show 'em all, she thought grimly. *I can handle this. I'm an adult. A mature professional.*

Through the cracks between her fingers, she glared at the too-handsome face that grinned up at her from the *Update*'s cover page.

I'm a grown woman and a widely respected executive. There's no reason why I should treat Jonas Riley any differently than I would any other colleague.

Lifting her chin from her hands, Cat grabbed a black felt-tip pen and began to initiate a few minor cosmetic changes that made viewing the photo, if not more enjoyable in the strictest sense, at least a lot more entertaining.

It's good to know my feelings for him are long gone.

Cat took out an eraser and rubbed out the ink in Jonas's eyes, à la Little Orphan Annie.

And that I truly have gotten on with my life.

With great satisfaction, she surveyed the addition of pointy horns, blacked-out teeth, and a bulbous, hairy nose wart. Soon she was scribbling alternately with three different pens. After what felt like two or three minutes, the grotesque makeover was complete.

"There," Catherine exclaimed, eyeing her hideous masterpiece with gratification. "Perfect." Her uncharacteristically childish impulse satisfied, she folded up the paper and stuffed it into her wastebasket. Then, acting on another silly whim, she fished the first page out of the trash, folded it neatly, and tucked it away in a stack of papers to be filed at a later date.

Her mission accomplished, Cat picked up her Time Champion and headed out the door to her next appointment, overwhelmed with gratitude that she no longer had any feelings, whatsoever, for the man who had once broken her heart.

TWO

"Five more minutes, Daphne," Catherine mumbled under her breath. "Five more minutes—and you are officially out of a job *and* one older sister." Perfectly trimmed, French-manicured nails tapped out a nervous rhythm on the expensive leather briefcase that lay across her slender knees. Beneath the fabric of her tailored wool-crepe suit and silk blouse she felt the skin on her back and arms begin to grow slightly damp.

Davis Pierce smiled encouragingly from his position in one of the artsy one-armed chairs in the Apollo Athletics lobby. "Relax, beautiful. The meeting doesn't start for another ten minutes. She'll be here."

"I'm tired of covering for her." Cat felt her frustration rise, imagined it was her blood pressure. "If it's not one thing, it's another."

"Aw, cut the kid some slack." Davis sounded unconcerned. "She's not that bad. Didn't you say she had a good reason for not bringing you the files the other night?"

"Just that she took them to my office and not my house." *If you call that a reason.* Catherine had been frustrated with Daphne before, but today her wrath was at an all-time high. A personal best.

"A natural mistake," Davis said generously. He seemed more than willing to dismiss Daphne's transgression. But then again, Cat thought, how far could she trust the opinion of a man who wrote important information on the palm of his hand? "Most people do work at the office, you know," he was saying. "Unlike you, most people don't actually consider reviewing client accounts a good time. You really should get a life, Cat. For example," he said, sitting forward eagerly in his seat, "this Friday night—"

"Down, boy."

"Oh, all right. All right."

As she had done countless times since their arrival ten minutes earlier, Cat allowed her eyes to wander over the strangeness of the sprawling lobby. The two side walls were painted a deep sapphire blue and covered with what appeared to be small neon-colored stones to create an athlete's "rock-climbing" structure. On the back wall hung a ten-foot replica of the company's nondescript sunburst logo—a reference to the ancient Greek god Apollo, and one of the first items Catherine planned to change if she got the account. Just in front of the wall sat a jet-black receptionist's desk constructed from galvanized rubber and designed in the shape of an immense running shoe. Cat tried not to stare.

Averting her gaze, she momentarily made eye contact with a well-dressed man in his twenties who sat several feet away, speaking in animated whispers to the sleek-looking brunette at his side. Then her attention shifted to the main entrance as she searched in vain for some sign of her sister's familiar curly brown head. In less than seven minutes, Cat, Daphne, and Davis would be called upon to pitch their campaign to Apollo's entire staff of vice presidents. It was the sort of opportunity that made or broke companies. And if Daphne, one of the Salinger Agency's top account executives, didn't arrive in . . . less than *six* minutes, now, Catherine and Davis would be forced to make the presentation without her.

She sighed dramatically.

"Poor little Cat," Davis sympathized. "You're really suffering, aren't you?"

"You make it sound like I need to be put to sleep." She crossed her legs, then quickly uncrossed them again in an uncharacteristic show of nerves. "This happens all the time. I'm early to every event I ever attend, while Daphne always shows up late. When is she ever going to change?"

"Probably about the time you stop expecting her to."

"Meaning?"

"Meaning you're just as stubborn as you make Daphne out to be. You probably drive her just as crazy too."

"Really? You wouldn't tease me?"

"You know, you might try cutting her some slack," Davis suggested, ignoring her attempts at sarcasm. "She's living her life the best way she knows how. And I happen to think she's not doing that bad a job of it. Maybe she's already started to grow up and you just haven't noticed."

"Oh, Davis, I doubt that," Catherine said wearily. "Look at your watch. The meeting is going to start any time now. I've said it before, and I'll say it again: The girl is trying to give me a nervous breakdown."

"You've told her to be early before, and it hasn't happened yet. What is it they say in Alcoholics Anonymous?" he wondered out loud. "Something about insanity being the act of doing the same thing over and over again, always hoping for a different result?"

"Well, if I'm not *already* insane," Cat complained loudly, "Daphne's certainly doing her best to make me that way." Hearing her words and the sharp sound of her voice, the young man across the room threw her a look that indicated he thought she might, in fact, be a bit touched in the head.

Catherine shrank back in her seat. *Thanks a lot, Daphne.*

31

Nutso. That was the sort of thing people generally thought about her youngest sister, not Cat. She didn't like the feelings the look elicited.

"You feel responsible for Daphne." Davis nodded knowingly and scratched his chin for effect.

"Thank you, Dr. Pierce." Cat gave a quiet laugh. "Tell me again, how much is this analysis going to cost me?"

"It's on the house. Your mind fascinates me. Someday I'll let you analyze me. If you're lucky," he said with a playful leer. "But for now, why do you think you feel this sense of responsibility toward your sister?"

"It's no big secret," Cat said reasonably. "It's just that *someone* has to watch out for Daphne. No one else does—not even Daph herself. She's just . . . well, flaky. And vulnerable. Every week she's got a broken heart, and every week it's been crushed by a different guy. The only thing I break on a weekly basis is my nails. She needs to be around someone who's responsible."

"And 'being responsible' is what you do best." It was not a question.

"Let's just say I've had a lot of practice." Catherine stood abruptly and wandered several feet away, effectively ending the conversation.

For crying out loud, Davis, she thought uncomfortably as she examined a poster on the wall. *What a terrible time to try to dig into my soul.*

But his words rang true: Being responsible *was* what she did best.

Cat had been only ten years old when she and her younger sisters—ranging in age from four to eight—lost their mother to leukemia. Though their father loved them fiercely in his own way, he had not been prepared to be father *and* mother to a houseful of little girls. Absorbed with his own issues—grief over the loss of his wife and a sense of responsibility toward Salinger & Riley, the advertising agency he had formed with Miles Riley—he had left the children in the care of hired housekeepers much of the time.

The housekeepers had done just that—kept the house. The actual task of mothering the three youngest girls had fallen largely to Cat, a role she undertook with great seriousness and energy. She had promised her mother she would help her father take care of the family. And even then, she had been a child who took her responsibilities seriously.

Keeping an eye on gentle, easygoing Felicia had been a breeze. Even mischievous Lucy somehow managed to stay out of serious trouble most of the time. But "daffy Daphne," as the kids at school had often called the baby of the family, had been a handful—and Catherine could not help seeing her that way still.

Growing up, none of the younger girls had been thrilled about answering to their big sister. Particularly as teens, the girls had complained that Catherine was nosy and controlling. But Cat knew they needed her and had done what she thought was right.

Professionally, if not relationally, the experience had served her well. As she grew, leading others had become second nature. Only eight years after graduating summa cum laude from the University of Southern California, she was at the helm of her father's ad agency, one of the strongest in Los Angeles, if not the nation. Even before his death, she had quickly risen through the ranks, reaching the level of vice president nine months before.

There was no question in anyone's mind that Catherine was the right woman now for the job of company president. She was the hardest-working executive at the agency. Everyone respected her. To her secret delight, some even feared her. Cat was successful. She was admired. She was powerful. She was . . .

She was hopping mad. "Where, in heaven's name, is Daphne?" Cat sighed again, louder this time and just a bit raspy, for effect.

"Have patience," Davis urged. He folded his arms behind his head and leaned back casually in the absurd-looking chair—the picture of relaxation. If it were not for the Brooks Brothers suit he wore, he would have looked more like a college student than a professional executive with a six-digit income.

"It looks like we're on our own," she said grimly. "Can you believe it? For the past two weeks, the entire staff's been working night and day on this dog-and-pony show. Apollo is one of the most lucrative corporations in the world. It's our job to convince them that we're the cutting-edge agency they want to take them into the twenty-first century. And Daphne is going to *miss* the whole thing."

"Down, girl," he parroted her earlier admonishment.

"All right. All right," Cat echoed his reply.

She had just rejected the idea of calling her sister on her cell phone—though Daphne carried one at Cat's insistence, she had not once remembered to turn it on—when the object of her wrath finally decided to make an appearance.

Cat's eyes opened a bit wider as Daphne puffed her way through the glass door to Apollo Athletics's main entrance. With both arms she clutched her enormous black backpack-style purse. Though it was designed to be worn on the back, as an item of clothing, Daphne usually forgot to throw it over her shoulder and was often seen carrying the gargantuan leather item close to her chest like a sack of groceries—a reasonable comparison, considering the bag's unwieldy size.

Catherine groaned. Even on workdays, Daphne followed

her own rules of style. Today was no exception. Company policy called for her to wear slacks or a skirt, at the very minimum. Instead she wore black boot-cut jeans and a sleek, deep-purple silk blouse with an open collar. A sheer, rose-colored scarf was tied at her throat.

But Catherine could lower her standards enough to accept the jeans and shirt, which were actually not that unusual for "creative types" in the advertising industry. It was the shoes—Daphne's horrible, nightmarish shoes—that caused Catherine's eyes to bulge open in disbelief.

She blinked repeatedly, but when she focused again the eyesores were still there. At the end of each of Daphne's stylishly clad legs was something that to Catherine looked like nothing so much as a muddy schnauzer. After several long moments of gawking, she finally recognized the fashion "don'ts" as her sister's pair of worn-out Apollo running shoes.

Daphne stopped and peered around the room before grinning and moving toward Cat. As she approached, she flapped one arm in the air, making a great show of panting and trying to catch her breath. Catherine absently smoothed her own charcoal-gray suit in an unconscious attempt to pull her sister together by proxy.

"Hi, Kit-Cat!" Daph said brightly, employing her sister's much-hated childhood nickname. "Hi, Davis."

"Hello, sunshine."

Taking a deep breath, she lowered herself heavily into an unoccupied seat beside her sibling. From across the room, the man who had earlier given Cat a look of sympathy now gave Daphne a look of obvious appreciation.

"Sorry I'm late," she said easily. "Are you guys ready?" Without aid of compass or map, she began to dig in her purse.

Catherine gave her a long, even gaze. "Daphne. What can you be thinking?"

The excavation of the backpack continued for several moments until Daphne stumbled upon the object of her search: a jumbo-sized packet of cinnamon-flavored gum. She grabbed a stick for herself, then offered the pack to her sister.

Catherine just stared.

"Okay," Daphne said easily, cramming a piece into her open mouth. "If you don't want one, that's fine—oh." She stopped chewing abruptly and nodded as she interpreted the meaning of Cat's gaze. "No gum in the meeting. Gotcha. Sorry. I wasn't thinking." She spat the offending piece of mangled, wet gum back out into her open hand and crammed it back in the wrapper, to be enjoyed at a future time and date. "I suppose gum wouldn't be appropriate—"

"Appropriate?" Cat struggled to keep her voice low. "*Gum* wouldn't be appropriate? Daphne, honey, look at your *shoes.*"

"Great, huh?" Daphne smiled so brightly, she practically glowed.

"Daph, they look like they've been through a war."

"And they still survive. Beautiful testimony, isn't it?"

Cat seized the straps of Daphne's pack and dragged it off her knees. "What have you got in here?" she asked, unhooking the top flap and peering inside. "Any boots you can change into? Black shoes?"

"Sorry, no. What's the matter? You're not quite catching the vision, are you?"

"No, I am not 'catching the vision.'" Though she expected to find tubes of melted lipstick and half-eaten Twinkies, Cat was surprised to find the contents of the purse neatly organized. "And I seriously doubt that the vice presidents of Apollo Athletics will be amused by your choice of footwear."

Daphne looked at her carefully. "They're just shoes, Cat. And I really think they'll like them. Anyway, don't you think you're taking this a little, um . . . seriously?"

"What's not to take seriously?" Cat stared at Daphne as if she were a stranger. "Don't you want to take care of the company Daddy spent his whole life building?"

"Well, of course I do."

"Don't you want us to get the Apollo account?"

"That's what we're here for," Daphne said gamely.

"Don't you want to keep it out of the hands of those mutants over at the Riley Agency?"

"Ye-es," the younger woman responded hesitantly. "I mean, I do want us to get the account. But aren't you taking this Hatfield and McCoy thing a bit far? We're not talking about the Capulet Agency or Montague & Associates, you know."

Catherine stared at her incredulously. *Blasphemy. Sacrilege.* But she didn't know why she was surprised. Daphne rarely took things—*any* thing—seriously. And yet she had thought that even carefree Daphne understood how greatly their father had been hurt by his best friend's betrayal twelve years earlier.

It had happened while Catherine was attending USC. All four girls were living at the family home in the Hollywood Hills, but it had been oldest daughter Cat in whom Edward had confided what was happening in his personal life and business world.

Since his early days in the advertising business, her father had worked with his closest friend and writing partner, Miles Riley. But in 1986, after their agency had been well established, Cat's father noticed that Miles was acting strangely. He seemed more driven, hungrier for financial success. And then one day Edward received a phone call from a client. It seemed that Miles Riley had approached the client and asked him to sign exclusively with Miles . . . not with Edward.

The company disintegrated shortly thereafter. By the time Cat's father realized what was happening, most of his clients were gone. Some had been stolen by Miles. Others had moved to other, "more stable" agencies. With one daughter in college and three more on their way, Edward Salinger had been forced to rebuild his business from scratch.

"I don't think all the Rileys are bad," Daphne was saying naively.

"Oh, really?" Cat said, her tone desert-dry.

She remembered clearly the Rileys' visits to her family's home when she was growing up. There had been a younger boy, Elliott, whom she'd had to watch over periodically when Miles and her father were working together. But it was Jonas Riley who haunted her memories. Strikingly handsome and tall, with a dry sense of humor—in every way like his charming father—Jonas had drawn her attention as though he were a red-hot flame and she a helpless moth, unable to tear herself from the fire.

Daphne and Lucy had been too young to care about Jonas in any context other than that of a much older brother. They had focused their energy instead on torturing poor Elliott, who gamely allowed the girls to lead him around, bossily calling him "husband." It was never clear to Cat which of the girls was supposed to be paired off with him . . . or if the two were taking turns at trying their hands at marriage. Possibly they themselves were unclear on the concept, not having closely observed a marriage in action since their mother's death. But since Elliott was not old enough to pose an actual threat as bigamist, Cat left the younger children to their harmless play.

The adoration she felt for Jonas seemed to Catherine to be

much less harmless. Both she and Felicia were smitten with the young man, who was three years older than Cat and six years older than Fee. However, boy-crazed Felicia's feelings were directed not just at Jonas, but at any male within flirting distance—and countless numbers *not* within flirting distance.

Felicia loved the Hardy boys.

Felicia loved *The Dukes of Hazzard.*

Felicia loved Gopher from *The Love Boat.*

Felicia was a very loving little girl.

But Cat's devotion for Jonas as she grew a little older was of the "I-must-have-him-or-I-will-die" variety. Page after page in her diary was filled with lengthy stories about her feelings for him. She adored him, at first, from afar. And he was infinitely *adore-able* in her eyes. She loved the way he would stand with his father, listening as Miles and Edward spoke about business matters. Though he was much younger than the two men, Jonas seemed able to relate to them as peers. Often he would throw his arm around Miles's or Edward's shoulders and laugh at some little joke one of the men had made. Cat loved the way her father's eyes lit up whenever the Rileys came over. Their frequent visits seemed to fill a void in his life; to provide him with masculine companionship he sorely needed in his household of girls, to give him a camaraderie from which he could draw enjoyment and strength.

And then one day—miraculously, it seemed to her—Jonas was looking at her as something more than just the daughter of his father's friend. And almost before she knew what was happening, they were a couple. For her and Jonas to be together in those days had seemed as natural and inevitable as breathing. Though they were young, their love was intoxicating and powerful, and Cat—like everyone else—had assumed they would eventually marry.

But then came Miles's betrayal. And as the agency fell

apart and the two older men's friendship ended, Catherine's relationship with Jonas unraveled as well.

She was not sure which had hurt worse in those days—seeing her father's pain, or feeling the loss of Jonas in her own young life. Her anger had many targets: Miles, of course, for hurting her father. Jonas, for many reasons, not the least of which was being so like his father—how could he not be just as untrustworthy? And, most of all, herself, for being foolish enough to care for anyone who would betray her.

She had vowed then never to allow herself to be taken in again. And she had succeeded. At thirty-one years old, she was a testament to the ability to keep oneself emotionally intact. Though she had gone on occasional dates, never again had she given her heart. She was safe. As safe as she could be.

She was also incredibly lonely . . . thanks to the Rileys.

And Daphne didn't think the family was all that bad?

"Come on, Cat." Daphne waved one hand dismissively. "Don't get all huffy. You're just in a snit because I was late. Seriously, don't you think this whole vendetta thing has gotten out of hand? I mean, it's one thing to be the best we can be. I'm all over that. But I don't think we should be competing against the Rileys. Let's forget about them. This isn't a game, you know. It's not a race. Why do we have to be out to get them? *They're* not out to get *us*—"

"Oh, I don't know about that." Catherine remained unconvinced. "They're after the Apollo account, aren't they—and they've moved back to town just to go after it. Who knows what they'll go after next? Remember who we're dealing with here."

"Oh, please." Daphne made a decidedly unladylike noise with her lips. "Now you're just being paranoid. We don't have the Apollo account yet. Half the agencies in the city are going after it. The fact that the Rileys want it, too, has nothing to do with us. Let it go, huh? Just because Miles was a big stinker to Daddy doesn't mean the whole bunch of them are slime-buckets."

"Maybe they are not all, as you say, 'slime-buckets,' " Cat allowed reluctantly, "and maybe they are. But this isn't the time to get into it. I think we should focus on the meeting."

"That's the best idea I've heard all day." Davis slapped his thigh and sat forward in his seat, clearly relieved at the prospect of a truce. "For a moment there, I thought I was going to have to get some mud, throw you two into a ring, and sell tickets."

"You wish." Cat grabbed her day-planner and began to dig for her notes about the Apollo bid. "Okay, let's get started."

She spent the next several minutes filling Daphne in on some details she and Davis had covered in the car on the way over from the office. She was just about to begin a review of the order of presentation events when she suddenly became aware of a figure standing, motionless, several feet behind Daphne. Catherine glanced up . . . then froze.

For a moment she simply stared, her mind overwhelmed with feelings of both anticipation and dread. Speechless, she looked up into the face she had hoped never to see again.

"Jonas!" Her mouth fell open, foiling any attempt she might make at appearing cool and composed. Hastily she scrambled to her feet, her agitation and discomfort too overwhelming to allow her to remain seated.

He was every bit as gorgeous as she remembered. Jonas had always been in good shape. But his six-foot-one-inch frame had filled out in the years since she had last seen him, and he seemed to command even more attention than he had in his twenties. Jonas's manner of dressing had always been loosely stylish and generally casual. Catherine had rarely seen him wearing anything more formal than cotton twill pants and a heavy crewneck sweater. But that had been years ago. Apparently even Jonas had grown up, at least in that sense. Today he wore dark dress slacks, a crisp white shirt buttoned up to his strong, masculine neck, and a black-and-brown houndstooth jacket that brought out the rich color of his dark eyes. Only his crazy-patterned, multicolored tie thumbed its nose at convention.

Even his thick, dark hair was tailored, cropped neatly where it had once grown wild, making him even more attractive than before. Catherine felt the sudden urge to run her fingers through its inviting waviness. She looked away, embarrassed at the thought. But Jonas didn't seem to notice the blush she felt creeping up her neck and into her cheeks.

"Why, it's my little Cat!" he exclaimed, looking perfectly delighted to see her. A tiny smile crept to her lips, unbidden. Something stirred inside her and, in that moment, she fought two competing urges: to turn away in fear . . . and to throw herself into Jonas's arms.

Seemingly unaware of her mental and emotional dilemma, Jonas reached out and took her small hand between both of his own. "Listen, Cat, I was so sorry to hear about your dad. I kept meaning to write a note, to call. But, well . . . I wasn't sure you'd want to hear from me after all those years. . . ."

She barely heard his words. At the touch of his fingers, she had felt a delicious warmth creep over her skin. Cat tried not to sway under the contact, and in a moment the modified handshake was over. She felt a little dizzy as Jonas's hands withdrew, and she reached down to clutch the arm of her chair for support.

Jonas turned to her sister. "Daphne," he said with a smile that was only slightly less enthusiastic . . . and oddly familiar. "It's good to see you . . . again." Catherine thought there was something odd about the way he said 'again.' Was it her imagination, or was Daphne giving Jonas a strange look? Her expression seemed to communicate . . . what? Discomfort? Or warning. Cat's heart surged with pangs of jealousy and mistrust as Daph exchanged glances with Jonas. She suddenly realized that, as much as she tried to involve herself in her sister's life, she didn't *really* know what was going on in, or *who* was a part of, Daphne's world outside of office and family.

The thought was strangely unsettling. She'd have to remember to talk with her sister about associating with appropriate people. And Jonas Riley was definitely *not* appropriate. He was a Riley. He was the enemy. Besides, with that wide smile and those dancing eyes, he was much too dangerous. Daphne would never be able to hold on to her heart. It was hard enough for Catherine herself to do so. Even now, despite her long-held antipathy toward him, she felt an emotional tug that pulled at her soul.

Jonas extended a hand to Davis Pierce. "Jonas Riley." He threw a sidelong glance in Cat's direction as if assessing her relationship to the man.

"Well. The *legend* himself." Her associate grinned. Somehow, coming from him, the words did not sound presumptuous. "It's a pleasure. Davis Pierce." Jonas returned the friendly smile.

Catherine felt herself becoming distinctly nauseous at the sight of the two making nice-nice. "Well!" she said, her voice sounding thin and strained in her own ears. "My goodness, Jonas. Isn't this strange, running into each other after all these years." She scrambled to find words, any words, to fill the awkward space. "Isn't it? Strange?" The pitch of her voice was higher, the speed more rapid, than usual. Daphne gave her an odd look. "Seeing each other at Apollo Athletics, of all places. I suppose I know why you're here. You . . . we—"

Catherine's eyes opened wide. In her dismay at seeing him, she had nearly forgotten how dangerous he could be not just to her sister, but to her company. Her eyes narrowed suspiciously. Suddenly Jonas looked even more menacing than she previously had considered him to be.

"Wait a minute. Exactly how long have you been standing there?" She tried desperately to remember what she'd been saying about their ad strategy before Jonas walked in.

He raised his eyebrows almost imperceptibly at the change in her tone. "I just walked up a moment ago," he said simply. His dark eyes met hers without flinching. "Why do you ask?"

"How much did you hear?" Her look and tone were dripping with accusation. She did not even bother to try and hide it.

"Sorry?" Jonas turned his head to one side and blinked at her, like a scientist examining a particularly interesting specimen. "How much did I hear of *what?*"

Daphne was staring at her, open-mouthed. "Oh, for goodness' sake, Cat," she said in a low voice, sounding like a teenager whose mother insisted on holding her hand at the mall. "Stop being so ridiculous."

"What?" Catherine held her day-planner protectively against her chest. "Don't you think it's just a bit suspect, our running into him now, like this? He probably heard everything we were talking about. No doubt he followed us in here, to find out what we're up to." The man obviously had some sort of James Bond complex. Well, he wasn't going to get any information out of her!

"Excuse me?" Jonas looked thoroughly confused now. "Why would I follow you? And what *are* you up to?"

"So you admit it!" Catherine cried triumphantly.

"But I didn't say—"

"You admitted you wanted to know what we were up to."

"Yes, but I was only trying to—"

"I know what you were 'only' trying to do, *Mister* Riley," she said smugly. "But it won't do you any good. You aren't going to get a thing out of me."

"Obviously," he grinned, unshaken by her mood swing. "We've been talking for five minutes, and all I've learned is that you are a paranoid lunatic."

"Excuse me?" Catherine gaped at him. The Riley confidence was even more unshakable than she remembered. "Nice try, Jonas. But I know what's really going on here."

He looked helplessly from one woman to the other. Daphne shrugged apologetically but otherwise offered no assistance.

"Look," he said finally, directing his comments back at Catherine. "I know a lot has happened between us—and our families. But that's water under the bridge now. I wish you'd forget about what my dad did. I know it was rotten; I think he knows it too. But it doesn't have anything to do with me or my brother. I never wanted there to be a rift between our families." His tone grew gentle. "Or between *us*."

Catherine looked up into his face, though she knew she should turn away. Something burned inside her. How wonderful it would be if she really could believe him. . . . "Daphne here understands—" he continued.

Catherine blinked at the reference to her sister.

"Uh, actually, 'Daphne here' understands that we have a meeting to go to," her little sister interrupted nervously. She grabbed Catherine by the arm. "Look, it was nice running into you, Jonas," she said a bit too brightly. "Really. *Tell Elliott I said hello when you see him.*" She pulled Cat back down into the chair and reseated herself. "I'm sure we'll run into each other again," Daphne threw over her shoulder dismissively. "But right now, we really do have to prepare for our meeting."

Jonas looked confused but obediently backed away. "All right, then . . . I guess. I'll see you soon. *Both* of you." As he spoke these final words, he patted Cat's hand softly, leaving a tingling warmth that stayed with her even after he was long gone.

Shaken, she watched him move to the other side of the room and greet the man and woman she had observed earlier.

"Don't think about him, Cat," Daphne instructed her. "Forget about it."

Catherine nodded, but her heart continued to race. Forget about Jonas? As if she could. She'd been trying all morning . . . maybe even for years.

She eyed her sister curiously. Just minutes ago, Daphne had been defending the entire Riley family. Now she was practically ordering Jonas to get lost. Perhaps Daphne had taken her words to heart.

Perhaps.

Then again, perhaps she had not. For some reason, Catherine could not shake the feeling that something was going on. Something she did not understand. Something that, if she knew about it, she would not like at all.

Gathering her papers in hand, she determined to push Jonas out of her mind and to focus on the meeting. But before doing so, she gave in to the urge to give her nemesis one last glance.

After the way he'd been treated by her and Daphne, she expected to see him looking defeated. But to her chagrin, his face instead held a look of quiet bemusement. Though he was making small talk with his associates across the lobby, he was staring directly at her and Daphne, looking half-delighted, half-confused, and—if she was correctly reading the expression on his face—more than half-convinced that the mature, professional Catherine Salinger was totally out of her mind.

THREE

Jonas "fell" for Catherine on the night of their very first date —or so she had been fond of telling friends and acquaintances during the earliest phases of their courtship.

Thirteen years later, she still remembered the event as if it had happened only yesterday.

The invitation came casually enough. During one of the regular Riley family visits to the Salinger household, Jonas crammed his hands in his pockets and suggested innocently, "Hey, Cat. If you don't have plans already, maybe we could catch a movie later?" Not the declaration of love she'd fantasized about . . . but, she figured, it was a start. After she stammered out an affirmative response, Jonas went to join both their fathers in a heated discussion about ethics in advertising while Catherine flew upstairs to spend the next three hours breathlessly preparing—under the watchful eyes of Felicia, Lucy, and Daphne—for the date of her dreams.

Despite the singing of her heart ("I'm in Love with a Wonderful Guy"), she tried to keep her expectations relatively low. Jonas had flirted shamelessly with her for weeks but still had made no verbal declaration of interest. There was no way to know whether he had asked her out because he harbored romantic interest toward her or because he simply had nothing better to do that evening. Not that a popular UCLA senior like Jonas would have any trouble finding companionship on a Friday night. Cat suspected that only a case of head lice could possibly keep Jonas's women admirers away; and even *that* would likely draw hoards of nauseatingly tender-hearted nurturers to his side.

Still, he *had* asked, so Catherine felt fairly certain that he at least liked her. But to what degree—and in what manner—remained a mystery.

A mystery she would get to the bottom of that night . . . or die trying.

When he arrived later that evening, Jonas informed her that he had abandoned the idea of a movie. Instead, he proposed that they take a leisurely—and to her young heart, gloriously romantic—drive down the Pacific Coast Highway.

The whole evening was as magical as she had dreamed it would be. As the setting sun bathed the California surf in gentle hues of rose and gold, Catherine and Jonas happily exchanged meaningful glances and engaged in small talk about every subject imaginable, from politics to pet peeves.

He looked across the passenger compartment of the car with challenge dancing in his eyes. "Tell me one thing that really annoys you. And I mean *really* annoys you."

"Well . . . I'd have to say: people who want to know what annoys me."

"Hardy-har-har." Jonas eyed her with mock disapproval. "No, really. I'm serious."

"All right, all right. What really annoys me?" Catherine thought for a moment. *Men who don't kiss on the first date?* She reluctantly dismissed the idea of dropping such an obvious hint. She couldn't have Jonas thinking she was easy; nothing could be further from the truth. Although, if he *did* want to kiss her good night, she certainly wouldn't make it hard for him to do so. With each passing moment it was getting more and more difficult to keep her attention on their conversation and not the gorgeous, masculine face that was just inches from her own.

Cat cast a furtive glance in his direction, but Jonas's calm expression revealed nothing of his feelings for her, one way or the other. She watched with silent admiration as he maneuvered his classic 1967 Mustang along the historic highway. With unshakable confidence, he easily controlled the car's every move. As if it were a thinking, breathing animal, she thought, the convertible responded immediately to his every touch.

Jonas turned and caught Cat staring. Her cheeks burned hot. His smile deepened.

"I'm waiting," he reminded her, managing to sound both romantic and playful.

Catherine frantically searched her mind for a grown-up response. "Well . . ." She considered her answer thoughtfully. "I guess I hate it when people call me 'sweetie' or talk to me like a child, just because I'm still fairly young," she said, trying her best to sound mature. "That's why I'm looking forward to college so much. I think now that I'm almost twenty, people will treat me with more respect and finally recognize that I'm an adult."

Jonas's features twisted slightly, and he looked suspiciously like he might be trying to stifle a sneeze . . . or a laugh. "You're eighteen, aren't you?" he remarked.

With a squeak of her vinyl seat, Cat sat up squarely and fixed him with a level gaze. "Well, that's *almost* twenty!"

"Almost."

Her pulse quickened. "What's that supposed to mean?"

Jonas laughed and held up one hand in protest. "Nothing at all."

"You're saying I'm just a kid." The implication stung. "Admit it. You *are*." Catherine leaned back and stared out the windshield for several long moments, pretending to ignore him until the silence got to her at last. "You're not *that*

50

much older, you know," she grumbled.

"Three years," Jonas said reasonably.

"Old man."

"Gorgeous young babe."

Catherine grinned then, and so did he.

"Oh, my poor, itty-bitty Kitty-Cat. Such a *sweet* widdle thing—" Scrunching up his strong, masculine features, Jonas stretched out one arm in order to tickle her under the chin.

"Augh! Stop it!" Catherine pushed his hand away and then collapsed in a fit of laughter.

They drove for nearly a half-hour more before Jonas pulled in at a tiny, out-of-the way café known locally for its zesty shellfish stew and mouth-watering swordfish steaks. After a brief discussion, she and Jonas agreed to try the specialty.

They were not disappointed. The meal was delicious, the atmosphere of the beachfront dining room magical, and they talked late into the night—laughing and joking for hours within the circle of the candle's soft, honey-colored glow.

It was nearly midnight when Jonas at last took Catherine's hand and led her up the porch steps to her father's door.

"Good night." Catherine turned to him with eyes full of expectation. Purposely, she paused under the porch light and made a herculean effort to communicate with him using only her eyes. *Kiss me, Jonas,* she thought, attempting a come-hither gaze. *Come on, come on . . . kiss me. No, don't look up at the window. Daddy's not looking . . . for goodness' sake, kiss me good night!*

"Is there something in your eye, Cat?" Jonas leaned forward and surveyed one squinty lid with great concern.

"No, it's nothing. I'm fine." Her skin flushed hot as she felt his warm breath on her face. In her embarrassment, she lapsed into a more normal expression and resolved simply to gather up what dignity she had left and tell him good night.

And then, at last, Jonas looked at her—*really* looked at her—with what she was certain were the softest, deepest brown eyes she had ever seen. Time seemed to stand still as their eyes caught and held. Without warning, Cat experienced a strange yet delicious yearning sensation that began in the pit of her stomach and seemed to reach down to her very soul. When Jonas smiled a moment later, every ounce of strength seemed to drain from her body, and she wondered, crazily, how she was managing to remain on her own two feet.

She leaned forward a fraction of an inch, hoping that might give Jonas the encouragement he needed. To her great relief he moved then, too, taking one step forward, and as he spread out his arms, Catherine felt as though the very gates of heaven were opening up to her.

With the grace of a dancer, she glided into his powerful embrace. Warm arms closed around her, restoring her strength. With a rush of confidence, Cat tipped her face up invitingly, closed her eyes . . . and felt Jonas's cheek press against her own as he enveloped her in a solid bear hug.

A look of passion froze on her face as he thumped her gently on the back. *What is that? Is he burping me?*

A second later, Jonas released her and stepped backward, clumsily tripping over his own shoes. "Uh . . . thanks for a wonderful evening, Cat," he said, then fell silent, though it appeared as though he wanted to say more. He tried to slip one hand casually into his jacket pocket, missed, and wound up self-consciously patting his hip while trying, unsuccessfully, to look as though that was what he had intended to do all along.

Catherine's lips twitched, but she managed not to laugh outright. "Sure, Jonas . . . thank *you.*" She was still trying to figure out whether the short-lived show of affection had meant "I value you greatly and want to move slowly," or "I'd rather drink acid than allow your lips to touch mine" when Jonas began to step away.

"Well, good night then." Keeping his eyes trained on hers, he waved nervously while inching his way back toward the cement steps . . . and, with all the poise of a vaudeville comedian, proceeded to stumble and trip his way down all six.

And that's when she knew.

Catherine smiled victoriously. Jonas Riley was smitten. He had, in the most literal sense, fallen for her.

And life would never be the same again.

"Cat? *Cat?*" Daphne quietly hissed.

"Huh?" Catherine raised her head from the notes she was pretending to peruse.

"It's time. They're calling us."

Cat spun around in her seat. Near the monstrous shoe-desk she spied the source of the summons: a young, dark-haired woman wearing a short, black suit, ivory blouse, jet black stockings, and—she had to look twice to make sure her brain was registering the image correctly—neon green Apollo sneakers. The woman's legs were long and slim, and she walked with all the poise of a runway model, seemingly unaware of the ridiculous picture she made in her professional attire and fluorescent running shoes.

Those shoes. Those horrible shoes.

Davis snickered. Daphne beamed. Cat groaned.

"Not a word about the shoes, Daphne," she whispered hoarsely, reaching to gather her things. "And I mean it. I have photos of you wearing braces and headgear, and I'm not afraid to use them."

The three strode quickly toward the opposite side of the lobby. With great effort, Cat managed to keep from looking directly at Jonas, though she remained painfully aware of his presence in the room. She very nearly breathed a sigh of relief when she, Davis, and Daphne reached the woman who had called for them. Soon Jonas would be out of sight, if not out of mind.

The secretary parted her cherry-red lips. "Mr. Jonas Riley?" she called out cheerfully.

Mr. Jonas Riley? Catherine's eyes flickered to the mouth that had uttered the enemy's name. "I'm sorry." Though she held tightly to her air of outward calm, her heart was fluttering like a schoolgirl's. "I believe there's been a misunderstanding," she gently explained in a voice that said "We all make mistakes." "Mr. Riley is not a member of our team. Salinger & Associates will be represented by Ms. Daphne Salinger, Mr. Davis Pierce, and by me. No one else."

The woman fixed Catherine with a cold-eyed stare. "Yes. I *know*. Mr. Riley is with the other group that will be participating in this morning's meeting."

"The other group?" Catherine shook her head, her expression a blank. "I'm sorry. I don't understand."

The woman's attitude quickly transformed from one of simple irritation to that of full-blown impatience. "You do know, don't you, that representatives from several agencies will be visiting with us today?" She spoke slowly and enunciated carefully, as if communicating with a small child.

Catherine gave a coolly professional nod while silently imagining ways to wipe that smug look off the woman's perky face. "Certainly I realize that. That is, I know there will be six companies making bids. I wasn't aware, however, that all the presentations would be taking place today."

So that was it! Jonas was here to make his own bid. And the group of people he was with must be employed by the Riley Agency. She felt anger rise within her once again. No wonder he had been standing behind Daphne listening! He clearly thought he could glean some insights about their presentation before either she or Daphne noticed he was there. What was it her sister had said? *I don't think all the Rileys are bad . . . they're not out to get us.* Cat's mind raced furiously. Jonas's actions had simply proven her point. He and his family were not to be trusted.

"I understand what you're saying," she patiently assured the woman. "However, as I said, Mr. Riley is not a part of *our* group."

"No, he's not. As *I* said, he's part of the other group that will be participating in this morning's meeting."

"You mean, with *us?*" Daphne's look of horror matched the feeling Cat felt growing within. "He and his group are going be in the conference room with us while we're making our presentation?"

The woman nodded.

"Yikes." Even Daphne seemed to pale at the prospect.

"So *two* groups will be making a presentation at one time? Each in front of the other?" Catherine kept her voice even and her manner composed.

"Yes," the woman explained wearily. "There will be a total of three meetings, each with two of the advertising agencies participating." She carefully scrutinized first Catherine, then Daphne. "Is that a problem for you?"

"Of course not." Catherine managed to sound unruffled. "My sister was just expressing her . . . surprise, that's all. You understand, it's not usually done this way."

"Well, it's the way *it's done* at Apollo Athletics," the woman told her, as if that settled it. "Our leadership group likes the way the process instills a sense of competition."

"Mmm." Cat nodded enthusiastically, the picture of understanding. She was determined to handle the situation like a professional, but she was finding it nearly impossible to keep her attention on anything but the muscular figure that had drawn near. Catherine still had her back turned to Jonas, but she knew he was now close. Even after twelve years, she recognized his scent: a unique mixture of soap, skin, and Old Spice cologne that was completely masculine—and entirely Jonas's own.

"Hello again, Cat," she heard him say with a voice smooth as honey. Then, more quietly, so that only she could hear: "I told you I'd see you again. But this is sooner than even *I* had hoped." Catherine drew in a sharp breath. Jonas was physically closer than she had realized; in fact, he had to be standing directly behind her. His voice rumbled loudly in her left ear, and she could feel the warmth of his breath on her cheek as he spoke. *Just turn around, Cat,* she told herself. *Return the professional greeting, then walk away.* Mustering all her courage, she spun on one heel to face him.

She swallowed hard. "Hello," she said, managing to keep her voice devoid of any emotion, then quickly forgot her resolve to turn from him. Jonas's familiar brown eyes were dancing. Despite her feelings of mistrust and anger, Catherine could feel herself being pulled into their depths.

Jonas looked nearly the same as he had a decade earlier. Life itself and its disappointments seemed not to have taken a toll on him. As she gazed into his eyes, Cat felt as though she was eighteen years old again. She pictured him again as the boy she had once known—carefree, enthusiastic, eager to make her happy. Eager to prove his love . . .

Abruptly, she turned away.

The woman eyed Cat curiously but said nothing about the exchange. "All right then," she announced, surveying the small group that had gathered behind Catherine and Jonas.

She gave the competitors a wicked grin. "It looks like we're ready to start.

"Let the games begin!"

As they walked into the meeting room, Cat managed to keep her back to Jonas at all times. A small snub, but it made her feel better nonetheless. She could see him, in her peripheral vision, hanging close. No doubt a ploy to wreck her concentration. Well! She would show him. As far as she was concerned, Jonas Riley didn't exist. From this point on, she refused to acknowledge his presence.

"Catherine." Leo Randolph, one of the senior vice presidents at Apollo, appeared at her elbow. "I understand you know Jonas Riley?" He indicated the man standing next to him.

Cat blinked. This wasn't happening.

Jonas gave her an innocent smile. He was enjoying her discomfort a bit too much. *Get a life, Jonas.*

"Yes, of course." She forced an even more enthusiastic—and, she hoped, even more natural—look of pleasure, then remembered the secretary's words: *Our leadership group likes the way the process instills a sense of competition.*

The smile slipped abruptly from her face.

Leo rubbed one hand across his shiny, bald head, seemingly oblivious to her discomfort. "Shall we all take our places then . . . ?" he said, turning away.

"Good luck," Jonas whispered. His breath was warm, his voice low.

"Keep your luck," Cat said stiffly. "*You're* the ones who'll need it."

His dark eyes flashed, and she thought she read a challenge there. "Touché." He grinned, then was gone.

Cat quickly found a seat as far down the table from Jonas as she could get and opened up her folder of presentation materials. She turned to see if Daphne was doing the same and found her staring at Jonas, too, as if willing him to look at her. Cat turned to watch the man who had caught her sister's attention and found her attention captured once more. The man oozed confidence; that, at least, hadn't changed. He seemed a bit harder, though. But then, maybe that was the case only with her. His presence unsettled her. Certainly she must irritate him as well. . . .

The thought delighted Catherine.

For several minutes, the room was filled with the sound of chair legs scraping against the floor. Cat reached over and squeezed first Daphne's hand, then Davis's. She felt Jonas's eyes bore into her, but tucked her chin down and focused her attention only on her proposal.

At last, Leo called the meeting to order. "To begin," he said graciously, "I would like to thank all of our talented guests for coming today . . ." Throughout Leo's little speech, Cat nodded and smiled in his general direction, trying to make eye contact whenever possible, all the while thinking impatiently, *Come on. Let's get this show on the road.*

After a brief introduction, Leo stepped down from the podium at the end of the conference table and returned to his seat. The smile still pasted on her face, Cat followed Leo with her eyes as he passed. The man was a bit annoying, she had to admit, but appeared to be a complete professional. She surveyed his stylish Armani suit, pin-striped shirt, blue-and-gold tie, and, as he drew closer . . . his glow-in-the-dark yellow Apollo shoes.

Cat swallowed hard. What was going on? Was it a conspiracy? Was giving up one's sense of professional style a requirement at Apollo?

Were all the executives wearing tennis shoes?

The thought at once intrigued and horrified her. Casually,

Catherine slid her ballpoint pen to the edge of the carefully polished table . . . and flicked it on the floor with a snap of her thumb and forefinger. Nervously she glanced around the table to see if anyone had seen her. No one had.

Except Jonas, of course.

He grinned.

She ignored him.

Throwing an apologetic look in the direction of Davis, who sat next to her and whose leg she had to reach past, Catherine leaned down to retrieve her pen. While reaching past her associate's feet, she quickly glanced under the enormous table . . . and counted nine pairs of Apollo shoes, including Daphne's.

What have I gotten myself into? These people are insane. . . .

"Catherine?"

"What?" Cat sat up like a shot, banging her head on the table. "Ouch!" Tears came to her eyes as she tried to focus. "Sorry. My . . . pen." She held up the offending object, wielding it like a hall pass.

"We're ready for you."

"Of course." Grabbing folder in hand, Catherine made her way to the front of the room. With sweaty fingers, she rubbed at the burning spot on her head, turned to the first page of her notes, then bestowed a political candidate's smile on the crowd. "Good morning," she began in a carefully professional voice that did not betray the rapid beating of her heart. "Thank you so much for allowing us to join you today. I can't tell you what an honor it is to meet with the leadership of such a fine organization. Not only are you an inspiration to the business world; you are the creators of what I think we'll all agree are the finest shoes on the market today. I use them during my own workouts and, as some of you may have noticed, my sister Daphne—also an account executive for

Salinger & Associates—hates to be without hers. In fact, I believe she's wearing them at this very moment!"

A murmur of approval echoed throughout the room as, one by one, the Apollo executives poked their heads under the table and took stock of Daphne's feet. For her part, Daphne simply appeared irritated to have been made the center of attention. Cat knew it wasn't Daphne's style to speak up; she preferred the subtler approach of following her gut and letting others respond to her actions. She never would have said anything about her shoes, would have instead just waited to see if the client noticed them. That was another of Daphne's many problems, Cat thought. She didn't know how to take advantage of an opportunity once it presented itself. Fortunately, one of them *did.*

She watched as Daphne cast another speaking glance in Jonas's direction. As the meeting progressed, she was beginning to feel even more strongly that Jonas and Daphne had seen each other recently and that Daphne was now trying to communicate something to him. She drew only a slight bit of consolation from the fact that the looks Jonas gave Daphne seemed to be ones of confusion. If she was trying to tell him something, he at least appeared not to be getting the message.

"In your folders, you'll find information about Salinger & Associates and some of the awards we've won recently. I believe you'll find that, like Apollo Athletics, we are a young, cutting-edge company full of fight and fire. We'll talk more about that later. But right now," Cat said hastily, "I'd like to introduce the woman who will be presenting Salinger & Associates' concepts to you today. I believe some of you know her already: Ms. Daphne Salinger."

As she made her way back to her seat, Catherine passed Daphne and gave her a subtle thumbs-up. The look she got in return was devoid of emotion.

However, by the time Daphne made it up to the podium with her laptop computer, from which she would run the multimedia presentation, her characteristic sparkle had returned. In fact, she looked downright mischievous.

Cat swallowed hard.

This wasn't good.

She tried to force herself to relax. After all, nothing was likely to go wrong. They had prepared a great presentation. The headlines were catchy, the concepts solid. And Daphne was a great presenter.

From its beginning months earlier, Cat had been proud of the campaign they had envisioned for Apollo Athletics. She pictured in her mind's eye the photos the execs would soon be seeing: sweaty, healthy-looking men and women engaged in a number of activities—running, bicycling, working out— while wearing Apollo Athletics shoes. At the top of each slide was the word: *Run.* At the bottom, in oversized letters, was the rest of the slogan: *For Your Life.* In the photos, it was clear that the athletes were putting their all into their workouts. But the artwork wasn't pretty, by any means. The images they had chosen were very strong graphically and tremendously inspirational. The focus of the campaign was not on style or beauty—though both were present in the ads—but on health. On taking care of oneself, in order to enjoy life more. That, Cat felt, was a campaign she could be proud of.

"As Catherine said, I'm here today to present some new concepts to you," Daphne began. She looked at Cat then, and a wicked glint appeared in her eye. "In fact, some of these concepts are so new, even my sister hasn't seen them yet."

Catherine bit her lip. This *really* wasn't good.

Her mind raced. She had to do something. But what?

As Daphne began to push buttons on her laptop, Cat knew it was too late. Someone dimmed the lights. Cat turned to a

61

screen near the front of the room and, to her horror, found herself looking at a cartoon of a huge, grotesque, drippy, red nose. Below it, the headline was printed in big, bold letters: "Some Things Were Just Meant to Run. Apollo Athletics."

Cat coughed, nearly choked. *No! This can't be happening.*

A loud, braying sound filled the room. Catherine immediately identified the rude sound as Jonas's outlandish laughter.

"Good heavens . . ." Davis's skin had turned the color of parchment. Cat felt the blood drain from her own face.

Eyeing her sister's expression, Daphne looked pleased. "Seriously, though," she began again, looking out over the roomful of dumbfounded executives.

"I love it!" Leo shouted.

"Wh-what?" Daphne eyed him curiously, not understanding. "Excuse me?"

"It's hilarious! Brilliant!" He started to chuckle. Then he started to howl. Pretty soon, tears of laughter were streaming from the eyes of all the Apollo Athletics executives.

Catherine looked around the room, stunned. They couldn't be taking the idea seriously. But obviously they were.

Daphne looked confused. "But it's a joke—" she began.

"—a joke whose time has come," Catherine added smoothly, coming to stand beside her sister.

"But, Cat," Daphne whispered. All around them, the raucous laughter continued. "I wasn't serious. It was a joke I was going to pull on you this morning, and I never got the chance. Even now, when I showed it to them, it was just supposed to be an icebreaker."

"Nothing we can do about it now," Cat hissed. "We're going to have to go with it.

"And may God have mercy on our souls."

FOUR

"I'm telling you, it was the worst day of my life!" Catherine complained.

Gratefully, she settled back against her cheap plastic lounge chair, planted in the hot sand near the beachfront home shared by sisters Lucy and Daphne. After her hectic midweek workday, she'd hated fighting the traffic all the way out to Malibu. But now that the she was here—and had changed from her sleek business suit into a comfortable white scoop-necked T-shirt and cut-off jeans—she was actually beginning to relax.

At least, as much as she ever did.

"Poor baby," Lucy dragged a second chair over to where Cat lay sprawled under the pleasantly warm late-afternoon sun. She, too, was dressed for the Southern California weather—in Pacific blue shorts, a celery-colored tank, and white espadrilles—and her mane of short chestnut curls bounced as she shook her head in evidence of her support. "Drink your iced tea and tell Miss Lucy all about it."

"Please." Cat drew her tortoise-shell sunglasses down on her nose and peered over the top of the tinted lenses. "Don't pull a big-sister trip on me, little one. I outrank you."

"My goodness," Lucy exclaimed, flopping down beside her. "Talking with you is like trying to soothe the savage beast. Would Your Highness like some music? Shall I peel you a grape?"

"Thanks for the offer," Cat shot back, deadpan, "but I'll

wait for dinner. Chez Olé, right?"

Every Wednesday night the four sisters met for an informal meal at one of the girls' homes. This week it was Lucy's turn to play chef, but earlier that afternoon she had called to explain that she just wouldn't have time to shop and cook and to ask if Cat would mind if they just ate out.

"I already checked with Felicia," Lucy said. "She doesn't care, as long as she gets out of the house. Robert's in another of his sulking moods." She didn't even bother to conceal the disdain in her voice. None of the sisters felt that Felicia's husband treated her anywhere near as well as she deserved. "We can still meet here," she told Catherine, "but I'd rather not ask Daphne to fill in for me."

"Amen to *that.*" Cat breathed a sigh of relief. The last time the sisters had met at Lucy and Daphne's, Daph had cooked—an odd-looking and even odder-tasting eggplant and cabbage affair. Her stomach still hadn't recovered.

"Daphne, uh, can't do it," Lucy said cryptically. "And even if she could . . . well, between you and me, I don't think I could survive another of her cooking adventures. I'm sorry about this, but do you mind terribly if we go to a restaurant?"

"You're asking me if *I* care?" Cat laughed. She herself hadn't had a chance to stop at the store in almost two weeks. She was out of milk, bread, potatoes—all her regular staples. At this point, in fact, her pantry held little more than tuna and a few cans of low-sodium soup. "I think we've ordered pizza the last two times it was my turn to host."

"That's true," Lucy agreed. "It's a shame too. You're a good cook."

"Don't waste your flattery, love. I already told you eating out would be fine. Besides, I'm having such a rotten week that even eggplant and cabbage would be the best thing that's happened to me."

"That's revolting. So what's the problem?"

Catherine sighed into the telephone receiver. "Oh, it would take too long to explain. I know you don't have time; you're as busy as I am."

All four sisters' lives were a whirlwind. Felicia spent all her energy raising two small children, attending social functions with her physician husband, and coping with the pain of Robert's neglect. The other three sisters were unmarried and worked at full-time business careers: Cat and Daph at Salinger & Associates, Lucy at the thriving video dating service she owned and ran in Santa Monica.

Though Cat had a hard time considering Lucy's "matchmaker" job a real profession, she knew her sister worked as many hours as she did, if not more. A local magazine's article on Lucy's service had brought her more than five hundred new clients in the last two months; apparently, she was the hottest thing to hit the dating scene since . . . since . . . good grief. Not having dated in so long, Cat had no idea what Lucy was the hottest thing since. Still, she was impressed, in spite of herself.

Lucy was silent for a moment, then offered, "Why don't you come up an hour early tonight and we'll talk?"

"I don't know." The long list of unfinished tasks on Cat's to-do list nagged at her. But Robin's comments the day before were nagging at her, too, churning up rare feelings of insecurity. "It might be good for me to get away from this zoo for a while and enjoy some relatively normal company. But I thought you didn't have time even to shop for food. I'm sure you don't have time to sit around visiting with your crabby old sister."

Cat could have predicted her sister's response. Good old Lucy. "No, I don't *have* the time," she conceded. "But for you, I'll make the time. Come on. When's the last time you came out just to see me?" Her tone turned to one of playful wheedling. "Don't you *looooove* me?"

Cat laughed. "Stop it. That's emotional blackmail."

"Uh-huh. Is it working?"

She sighed and smiled. "Like a charm."

"Six o'clock?"

"Save me some iced tea . . . and, honey, I am all yours."

By the time she had reached her sisters' house, Catherine was a basket case. Traffic on the Santa Monica Freeway had been a nightmare. Carol had called in sick after just one day on the job; Robin had been irritable and forgetful; Daphne had been avoiding her all day. Worst of all, since the disastrous Apollo meeting the day before, mental images of a grinning Jonas Riley had haunted her every waking moment—not to mention her nighttime dreams.

As soon as she arrived, Lucy had grabbed a thermos of Cat's favorite sun tea along with two tumblers of ice and a pair of tiny paper umbrellas, then led the way directly to the beach for something she called "ocean therapy."

As they lay side by side, breathing in great drafts of fresh sea air, Cat noted that the "therapy" did indeed seem to be causing the tension she felt in her neck to diminish.

"So where's your wacky roommate?" she said lightly, wriggling into a more comfortable position on the unsteady lounge chair. She'd stopped by Daphne's office at five o'clock, but her youngest sister had already left for the day.

Lucy shrugged. "Your guess is as good as mine. I rarely see her before bedtime. She doesn't use this place for much other than sleeping these days."

"Really?" Cat's antennae were up. The nagging ache in her neck returned for an encore. "She's always out of the office by five."

"Seriously? Man, I want *her* job." A short laugh escaped Lucy's lips.

Cat thought for a moment, couldn't let the question go unasked. "All right, I'll bite. If she doesn't come home, where *does* she go?"

"Lots of places, probably," Lucy said, sounding unconcerned. "I usually don't ask. Daphne's a big girl. She can take care of herself."

"Mmm." Cat watched as a group of young college students began an impromptu game of volleyball not more than twenty feet away. Though they couldn't be more than ten years younger than she was, she felt decades older. "I was thinking about this just the other day. I mean, I see Daphne constantly, but I don't know much about her friends, who she spends time with. Do you?"

"Some." Lucy settled her dark glasses on the bridge of her nose and reached for the sunscreen. Her expression and tone revealed nothing. Cat watched her closely. Was she being purposely evasive?

"But don't you think it's strange, our not knowing where she spends her time?" she pressed. "We're her sisters, you know. It's our responsibility to take care of her."

"Whoa, there. Where'd you get that?" The lotion belched its way out of Lucy's bottle and landed in her hand with a splat. "It's *Daphne's* responsibility to take care of *herself*. And it's God's responsibility to watch over her. Contrary to what you may believe, Cat, taking care of Daphne's life is not your job."

"I never said it was," Catherine huffed. "I just happen to think that one of the primary ways God watches over Daphne is through us."

Lucy raised one eyebrow and regarded Cat with a look of thinly veiled disapproval. "Well, la-dee-da. Rather presumptuous of you, don't you think?"

Cat felt her skin flush hot, and not from the sun. "I didn't mean it the way it sounded. I'm just saying that God uses people to take care of one another. Like family."

"Maybe so," Lucy conceded, rubbing sunscreen into her legs. "Makes a nice story, anyway." She looked innocent enough, not at all like a woman with a hidden agenda. But Cat was beginning to suspect that there was more to their little meeting than Lucy had led her to believe.

"What's that supposed to mean?" she said with just a trace of irritation. It didn't matter if she asked. She had a feeling Lucy was going to tell her, whether she wanted to know or not.

Lucy poured another handful of lotion and moved on to her knees. "It's just so conveniently . . . altruistic, don't you think? I mean, if that's your justification there's no real reason to apologize for being bossy, pushy, meddling—"

"All right," Cat muttered. "I get the point."

"—assertive, commanding, imperious—"

"Lucy." The look Cat gave her was anything but loving.

"—authoritative—"

"I knew I shouldn't have given you that thesaurus last Christmas," Cat said dryly.

"Admit it, Cat. You've always been a bit of a control freak."

"Says the woman whose job is to *choose people's partners for life.* You're a *matchmaker,* Luce. Talk about being a control freak. . . ."

"I only help people find each other; I don't push them to get together. I'm no Yente."

"And I'm no Stalin," Catherine insisted heatedly, Robin's accusation still echoing in her ears.

Lucy looked at her in surprise. "Whoever said you were?"

Cat sighed. "Don't ask."

"All right then. What's bothering you?"

"Nothing," she said hastily. "*Everything.* Oh, I don't know." Suddenly, Cat felt very confused. Perhaps the sun was causing her to dehydrate. She took a long drink from her glass of sweet tea. "Do you know, I haven't talked to Daphne since Monday night. I had to reprimand her after the Apollo meeting, and then she avoided me the rest of the day. I finally caught her and gave her the rest of the week off—told her to come back next Monday. She really has earned the break. Besides, I thought it'd give us both a chance to cool off. But now I've called her twice and she's not even returning my calls."

Lucy stopped rubbing lotion on her body and looked up. "Daphne's just been . . . out a lot. You can't take it personally, Cat."

"But it doesn't even make sense," Cat said. "*I'm* the one who has something to be upset about. I almost died of embarrassment on Monday."

"Yeah." Lucy grinned. "I heard about that. Oh, to have been a fly on the wall. . . ."

"It's not funny," Cat grumbled.

"Of course. You're right." Lucy drew her features into a more serious expression. "It must have been terrible, going through all that in front of Jonas."

Cat glanced away with what she hoped was an air of detachment. "Jonas who?"

"Jonas who?" Lucy snickered. "Now *that* is funny. How'd the old dreamboat look after all these years?"

Cat tried to maintain a look of dignity despite her sister's reaction. "Okay, I guess. I hardly noticed."

"Stop. You're killing me." Lucy held one hand to her side as if in pain from too much laughter. Cat didn't crack a smile.

"What? Oh, you're serious?" Lucy looked surprised, then dropped her hand and shrugged good-naturedly. "Fine. If you want to pretend you don't care about Jonas anymore, I'll pretend to believe you. I won't say a thing. Won't *do* a thing."

"Lucy!" Cat narrowed her eyes to mere slits. "Don't even *think* about it, little Ms. Matchmaker."

"Who me?" Lucy was the picture of innocence. She snapped the bottle of sunscreen shut and tossed it to Cat, who caught it easily. "I don't know what you're talking—"

"Yeah, yeah. Save it for someone who doesn't know your act," Cat said firmly. "Jonas and I are through and have been for a long time."

"If you say so."

"I say so."

"Okay, fine."

"Fine."

"Great."

"Great." Cat glared at her. "Do you want to hear the rest of the story or not?"

"I'm aquiver with anticipation."

Catherine proceeded to bend Lucy's ear with a version of events that she was certain would be much more accurate than any account that might have come from Daphne's lips. Lucy's reaction, however, left much to be desired. Though Cat fully expected her to show signs of shock and disapproval, Lucy simply appeared amused by the whole sorry affair.

"So how were things left?" Lucy asked when she was finally through explaining.

"Believe it or not—and I assure you, I'm having a hard time accepting it myself—the Apollo execs truly seemed to like Daphne's fake presentation the best. They want time to think it over." Cat clutched at her stomach. "I think I'm going to be sick."

"And what about Jonas's presentation?"

"Well, they liked it, too, though I couldn't tell how much." She fidgeted nervously with the little umbrella in her glass of tea. "It was fairly clever, I'll admit. Do you remember those little reading primers they used to have in elementary schools? The ones that said things like, 'See Jane run'?"

"Sure."

"Well, that was their first headline: "See Jane Run. Run, Jane, Run." Then they had all these images of a very athletic woman running—in the desert, up in the mountains, through the woods. All very inspiring. Blah, blah, blah."

"I'm fascinated. Really," Lucy said in a voice that expressed anything but fascination. "Now . . . tell me more about the juicy stuff. How was your old flame?"

Catherine hesitated for a moment before speaking. She didn't want Lucy to make a big deal out of what had happened, but she was dying to know what another woman thought. "That's the weird thing," she said at last. "Jonas acted sort of . . . I don't know . . . *distracted* during his presentation. Half the time, he wasn't even paying attention to his presentation or even the Apollo execs."

"And just what—or who—*was* he looking at?" Lucy asked mischievously, looking as though she knew the answer.

"Well . . ."

"Yeeeeees?"

"Oh, all *right*." Catherine sighed heavily. "He was looking at me a good part of the time. Is that what you wanted to hear, missy?"

"As a matter of fact . . . yes, it is," Lucy said, adopting a tone of playful superiority.

"I ignored him, of course—"

"Of course." Lucy echoed her serious tone.

71

"Don't get too excited, my little matchmaking friend," Cat warned her. "You're way off on this one. I'm telling you, I *don't* like the guy anymore. If I feel anything for him, it's contempt. And besides, half the time he was looking at Daphne too."

"Seriously?" Lucy sat up straight and looked at Cat. She had her full attention now. "How did Daphne respond?"

"Um . . . I think she was looking at him too."

Lucy's pretty round face switched from a look of teasing to one of compassion. "That really bothered you, didn't it?"

"No!" Cat denied vehemently, sitting up in her chair and almost spilling her tea. Lucy arched her brows in surprise. "No." Cat made a conscious effort to lower her tone. "It didn't bother me. I dated Jonas a long time ago. It's none of my business now *who* he looks at."

"Even if you think he's looking at your sister?"

For some reason she could not explain, the words made Cat's heart ache. She shook her head. "I don't *think,* I *know.* Forget it, Lucy. You weren't there. I was. I *saw* it. He was looking at her," she said stubbornly, then looked away, embarrassed. "Not that it matters."

"Oh, really?" Lucy sounded unconvinced. "Didn't you just say that it bothers you not to know where Daphne goes after work and who she spends her time with? Don't you think that maybe, just *maybe,* you're especially concerned now because you suspect her of having some kind of contact with Jonas Riley?"

"Don't be silly," Cat said stiffly. "My feelings have nothing to do with Jonas. And my only problem with Daphne is the fact that she's so irresponsible. She never should have pulled that stunt in our meeting."

"But it worked out in the end, didn't it?" Lucy said, sounding maddeningly reasonable.

"That's not the point," Cat argued patiently. Obviously, Lucy didn't get it. "It could have gone either way. The Apollo folks just as easily could have been angry with us for wasting their time. Daphne didn't know how they would react; she never should have taken the risk."

"You know, Cat, you said yourself that Daphne's been one of Apollo's main contacts all along. She probably just read the signals right. She got a feel for the tone of the company and played the game accordingly. You should give her credit for that, at least."

Cat knew she was right but could not bring herself to admit it. "Whose side are you on, anyway?" she asked testily.

"I'm on *both* your sides, silly."

Cat felt like a pouting child. "So when do you get to the part about defending *me?*"

"Been there, done that," Lucy said brightly. "I had a conversation just like this last week with Daphne."

"Mmm. I thought I felt my ears burning." Cat averted her gaze, looking out to the hazy brown horizon. "So, what terrible things did she have to say about me?"

Lucy smiled gently. "There's that paranoia we all love so much."

"Seriously . . ."

For as long as Cat could remember, there had been a power struggle between her and Daphne, though for reasons she did not understand the tension between them seemed to have increased in recent months. Perhaps Lucy could help her identify and solve the problem, once and for all.

"Sorry. I'm afraid I can't tell you anything." Lucy looked and sounded genuinely regretful. "Doctor-patient confidentiality, you know."

"You're not a doctor," Cat said irritably.

"Shows how much you know." Lucy sat up straight, but

did not succeed in looking any more dignified. *"I* am a doctor of *loooooooove."*

"You, my dear, are a doctor of *baloney."*

"Careful," Lucy chided. "You might need my services someday."

"I do just fine on my own, thank you."

"I can tell. When's the last time you had an honest-to-goodness date?"

Cat turned away in irritation. "No comment." Now Lucy was beginning to sound like Davis. Why was everyone so interested in her personal life? She saw no reason to pair up with a man just because everyone else expected her to. Sure, it would be great to love someone and to be loved in return. But she'd been down that road before, and it wasn't as easy as it seemed. There were no guarantees. She'd learned that, if nothing else, from her relationship with Jonas Riley . . .

Jonas. Cat tried in vain to push the image of him from her mind. Throughout the previous night, and all day long today, his look of amusement had haunted her. If only she'd known he would be at Apollo, she would have been better prepared. There's no way she would have allowed him to hear even one word of their planning session—not that it mattered, since he got to see the entire presentation anyway. Still, there were the man's principles to consider.

Jonas was obviously dishonest. He was also an awfully good actor. He'd actually had the gall to pretend he was shocked and confused by her mistrust of him! But how could she feel anything else? That she had once cared about him deeply didn't change the fact that she could not rely on him. That point had been made painfully clear after Miles betrayed her father.

Jonas had been talking with his dad about taking a job with Salinger & Riley after he graduated. Then, after the two men split, Jonas had decided to go ahead with the plans he'd made to work with his father.

"After all he's done?" she had cried at the time. "Don't do it, Jonas. I can't stand to see you working with him. Can't you see he's a terrible person? He hurt my father, and he'll hurt you too."

Jonas had remained unmoved. "Cat, you're talking about my *dad*. I don't like what he's done, but I can't change who he is to me. Whatever's happened, I won't run away. I have to stay and face it, to work through it. Whether you like it or not."

Cat *hadn't* liked it—not one bit. And their relationship had ended shortly thereafter.

"You know, you really could go easier on Daphne," Lucy's voice broke into her thoughts.

"Oh, really?" Thankful for the sunglasses that shielded her eyes, Catherine looked away. "Is that what Daph says when she comes home from the office?" Her voice was strained. "That I'm a big, bad meanie? That I'm an ogre to work for?"

"Still beating that dead horse, are you?" Lucy said, her voice calm. "All right, if you must know. She did say something about a poisonous apple and a talking mirror. I also seem to remember her talking about you huffing and puffing and blowing her cubicle down. Is that what you're looking for?"

"Shows how much you know. Daphne has an office, not a cubicle." Catherine could not help but smile, even if she was the target of Lucy's teasing. "All right then, smart aleck, I'll bite. What *are* you trying to say?"

Lucy eyed her evenly. "Just what I said—that you really are a bit hard on her. You've been hard on all of us, and I know it's because you love us. But you're even rougher on Daphne than you were on me and Fee. I'm not sure why.

Maybe it's because the two of you have such different temperaments. But I think it's partly, too, because you . . ." She hesitated.

"What? Because I *what?*"

Lucy looked at her nervously. "You won't like what I have to say."

"I never like what you have to say. That's never stopped you before."

Lucy grimaced. "Well, it's just that . . . Fee and I were both pretty well grown up before . . ."

"Before . . . ?" Cat prompted impatiently.

Lucy took a deep breath. "Before-you-started-dating-and-then-broke-up-with-Jonas." The words came out in a rush. "There. I said it."

"Yes, you did," Catherine said, sounding cross. "Now, what does it mean?"

Lucy reached out and squeezed her hand. "Oh, Cat! You've always been so good to us. You've been like a second mom, and we appreciate it. We *really* do. But things were different when we were younger. Before Jonas. *You* were different."

"How was I different?" Despite the heat of the afternoon sun, Catherine felt a slight chill.

"Well, you were a lot easier to get along with, for one thing." Lucy said. "You were a lot less suspicious. You took the world seriously then, but you didn't take *yourself* too seriously. What's more, you took the time to take care of yourself."

"But I—" Cat began. Lucy cut her off with an upraised hand.

"Yes, I know you still work out at the gym, but is that enough? After all, that's just a form of doing your duty, doing the right thing. But what about your hobbies? You used to read a lot. And you played tennis too. Nowadays, all you do is work and go to the gym and spend time with us. That's got to make your world pretty narrow, don't you think? Remember how you and Jonas used to go out and do things together with your friends? Maybe you should be doing that now. I know you have a lot to do now that Dad's gone, but maybe that's even more reason for you to get away from work for a while. Spend some time figuring out what you want to do. Get in touch with who you are as a person. Maybe spend a little time—" Lucy finally noticed the startled look on Cat's face. "Oh. Uh . . . sorry," she said sheepishly. "Did I say too much?"

"No. Really," Catherine said dully. "Don't beat around the bush. Tell me what you really think. I'd love to hear more."

"Oh, Cat!" Lucy laughed, but there was compassion in her voice. "I'm not trying to pick on you. I love you. We *all* do. Even Daphne. But we're not your responsibility, you know. You spend so much time worrying about us that you hardly take any time for yourself. Now, is that fair?"

"But I don't *need* to be taken care of," Catherine protested. "I'm fine. *You guys* are the ones who are all messed up."

"I appreciate that." Lucy chuckled. "But even if it's true, don't you think that's our problem? Your job is to love us, not to fix us."

"Lucy." Catherine sat up and leaned against her slim, tanned knees. "I'm not trying to *fix* Daphne. I'm just trying to keep her from making mistakes that will hurt her. You don't work with her. You don't see the way she dresses all quirky and unprofessional or shows up late or shoots off her mouth at the wrong times. . . ."

"No, I don't," Lucy agreed. "I just live with the girl. For

years, I saw the way she forgot to wash the dishes or pay the phone bill."

"Oh." Cat considered this. "So what do you do?"

"What I *used* to do is leave the dishes undone and let her phone get disconnected."

"But then, didn't she just want to use *your* phone?"

"Sure, but I wouldn't let her. It worked like a charm. Nowadays I don't have to say anything anymore. She's got things under control."

Catherine looked at her uneasily. "I don't get it. How is what you did different from what *I'm* doing?"

"Don't you see?" Lucy waved one arm in the air dramatically. "It's an entirely different thing altogether. *You* nag Daphne before and after she does things wrong, but then you cover for her when things happen as a result. *I* never said a word to her. But once the consequences came, I let her suffer."

"Sadist," Catherine said admiringly.

"Nag," Lucy grinned. The two sisters looked at each other for a moment in silent appreciation. "Seriously, Cat," her younger sister said finally, "I think you'll get a lot further with Daphne if you back off a bit. Let her take a fall if necessary, learn from her mistakes. Maybe you'll even find out she's wiser than you think."

"Do you think that'll work?" She tried to sound hopeful.

Lucy let out a sigh of exasperation. "The point *isn't* whether or not it'll work. You're not the one in control here, remember? The point is, you'll be recognizing Daphne as the adult she is. You'll be leaving responsibility for her life on *her* shoulders—and getting it off yours. Think of the freedom!"

Cat wasn't convinced. "But what if she makes some horrible mistake that I could have saved her from?" She drew in a deep breath. "What if—?"

"Admit it," Lucy said quietly. "You're still worried that maybe Daphne's seeing Jonas on the sly."

"I never was worried about that," Cat protested, staring down at her hands. "It's none of my business. And like you said, Daphne can take care of herself. She can—" She glanced up at Lucy and stopped in midsentence at the look of understanding she saw there. "Oh, all right. You win. Yes, it bothers me. I don't know why. It shouldn't. But I've been upset about it all day."

"Don't be. I'm certain there's nothing going on between Daphne and Jonas," Lucy said confidently.

"You are?" Catherine peered at her intently. "What makes you say that?"

"I live with the girl, remember?" Lucy said, raising her eyebrows for extra emphasis. "I *know* things."

"Really?" Cat perked up at that confession. "Like what? What do you know?"

"Oh, nothing really . . ." Lucy casually twirled one short corkscrew curl with her finger.

"Lucy!" Catherine looked at her meaningfully. She'd make her sister talk, even if it meant force-feeding her eggplant and cabbage. She was that desperate. *"What do you know?"*

"Look," Lucy said carefully. "I've already said too much. I can't betray Daphne's confidence. But—" She considered her options for a moment. "I think it's safe to give you this much: I know that Daphne is smitten with someone . . . and it's not Jonas."

Catherine let out the breath she hadn't even realized she'd been holding. "It's not?"

"It's not."

"You're sure?"

"Oh, I'm *sure.*"

Cat thought about this for a moment. "Oh." She tried not to let her feelings show, but could not keep a wide grin from spreading across her face. "How nice . . . for her," she said coolly. "That she likes someone, I mean."

Lucy pursed her lips and nodded. "That's sweet of you. I'm sure Daph would appreciate the sentiment."

"Okay, fine! I admit it. I'm relieved that Jonas isn't the guy she likes." Her eyes flickered away from Lucy's. "Those Rileys are trouble."

Her sister gave her a strange look. "Oh, I don't know about that."

"Now, don't you start defending them too!" Cat exclaimed. "I've gotten enough of that from Daphne."

"There are worse people one could love." Lucy spoke quietly. "That's all I'm saying."

"Ugh. That sounds like something Daphne would say too. You and your sister . . ." Cat grumbled. But her mood was much improved.

"Takes one to know one," Lucy shot back.

This time Cat didn't answer. Instead, she just lay back and finally allowed herself to enjoy the sunshine in earnest. She had just made a mental note to give Daphne a little space, as Lucy was advocating, when Lucy cleared her throat and said, "I suppose now is as good a time as any to tell you that it's just you, me, and Fee tonight. Daph's not going to make it to dinner."

Cat opened her eyes and looked at her sister sharply. "Why not? Is it because she's mad at me?" All feelings of compassion toward her youngest sister began to fade. "Is she *still* avoiding me? How mature is that?"

"Now, now, settle down," Lucy urged her. "It's nothing like that. She's just . . . busy, that's all."

"Busy doing what?" In Daphne's absence, Cat had no

choice but to make Lucy the focus of her interrogation.

"Um . . . I can't say," Lucy said quietly.

"Why not?" Now Catherine's suspicions were fully aroused again. "What's she doing? What's wrong?"

"Uh, Cat? Remember what I said earlier about being paranoid? Well, this would be a prime example—"

"Lucy!" Cat wished she could reach out and shake her. "If there's nothing wrong, then why can't she be here?"

"She had other plans, that's all."

Catherine scowled.

"Stop making that face. There's no reason to worry."

"I'm not worried."

"You *are* worried."

"All right," Catherine admitted. "But I have good *reason* to be worried."

"No you don't."

"Are you kidding? I have no idea where Daphne is or what she's up to."

"No, but *I do*. And I'm not concerned." But Lucy didn't look totally convinced.

Catherine rolled her eyes heavenward. "Now, why isn't that a comfort to me?"

"Cat, let this go." Lucy fixed her eyes on Catherine's and held her gaze. "Let Daphne go. Give her a chance to find herself, to *be* herself. Do you think you can do that?"

Cat looked at her forlornly. "Do chickens have lips?"

"No they don't. Let me try again: *Do you think you can do that?*"

"Oh, all right," Cat grumbled under her breath. "I'll try. But what is this world coming to? First Daphne asks me to stop disliking the Rileys. Now you want me to let go and trust Daphne to take care of herself—when we all know very well that she'll get her heart broken. Is the whole *world* going mad?" she exclaimed dramatically.

"Nope," Lucy told her, cheerfully plucking the tiny paper umbrella from her tea and raising the glass to her lips. "Just you, dear sister. Just you."

FIVE

"You did? You will? Uh-huh. Uh-*huh*." Catherine covered the telephone receiver with one hand while excitedly mouthing the word *Yes!* to Davis Pierce, who sat across the desk from her. It was fitting, Cat thought, that he should be in her office when the call came in from Leo Randolph concerning the next phase of the advertising firm's selection process. It was too bad Daphne wasn't returning her calls. She, of all people, should be there too.

"What's going on?" Davis whispered impatiently, leaning his elbows against Cat's big oak desk.

Keeping her hand over the mouthpiece, she spoke in the lowest voice possible: "We made the cut. They want to meet with us again this Friday, to talk further about our ideas."

Davis's eyes opened wide. He clasped his hands together and raised them over his head in a gesture of victory. Catherine grinned and nodded, then uncovered the receiver.

"Of course, Leo," she said in a smooth, professional voice. "That's not a problem at all. Two o'clock will be fine. Mmm-hm. And you'll be meeting with one other company that same day? Uh-huh. I understand. One other finalist. Will that be at the same time as our meeting?" She rolled her eyes heavenward, and Davis stifled a quiet laugh. "No. I see. Do you mind telling me who—?" She broke off as Leo interrupted her. "Daphne? Well, I'm not certain whether she'll be there or not."

Technically, Daphne's mini-vacation was over. She was

supposed to have been back at work on Monday, yesterday, but she hadn't shown up yet or even called. Not that Cat trusted her to behave herself at another meeting.

"Actually, she may be doing some research that afternoon that will help your campaign." It wasn't *actually* a lie, she thought guiltily. She didn't know what Daphne did when she was out of the office. For all she knew, Daph was going running on Friday afternoon in a pair of Apollo Athletics shoes. It *could* very well be true.

Then again, it probably was not. She felt a pang of conscience. Her reasoning was flawed, and she knew it.

"Uh-huh. Of course. Whatever you want, Leo. You're the client. Right. Well, thank *you*, Leo. We appreciate the opportunity to show you what we at Salinger & Associates can do. You bet. We'll see you on Friday, then. At two. 'Bye, now."

Catherine dropped the receiver back into its cradle and gave her colleague a look of triumph. "Well, Davis. There you have it. We're in for the next round."

"How many companies have they narrowed it down to?" he asked eagerly.

"It sounded like just two," Cat told him. "But it's hard to tell. Leo talks in circles. I know for sure that they're having a second meeting with one other agency on Friday. I couldn't get him to tell me which one, though."

She looked straight into Davis's soft gray eyes, and saw the look that told her he shared her suspicions. She opened her mouth, and the two of them grumbled simultaneously: "Riley."

"Ugh!" Catherine cried. "Can you believe it? It's got to be them. Everywhere I turn, it's Riley this and Riley that. Why does everyone think Jonas Riley is so great? I tell you, that man's really getting under my skin."

"I guess *so*." Davis gave her a strange look. "You really

hate those Rileys, don't you?"

His words brought Catherine up short. She blinked at him while considering what he'd said. *Hate.* There was no denying that her feelings toward Jonas were strong. But was what she felt really . . . hatred?

She quickly reminded herself that Jonas had already proved himself the scheming, ruthless competitor she had always assumed him to be. But when his face came to mind, all she could see was the soft laughter in his gentle brown eyes. She tried to imagine him within the walls of the Riley Agency, creating ad campaigns that were built more on style than substance—just like the Rileys themselves. But today, for some reason, she could not build an image of him in his business suit. Instead, she was flooded by memories of him in college, playing intramural football or beach volleyball. After games like these, he and Cat would often go out for pizza. She would laugh as she played with his thick, curly brown hair, and ask him again and again how on earth he had managed to completely cover his head with sand.

Her heart ached at the memories. Could she possibly hate a man whose very existence had once brought her such a sense of joy? No, hatred was not what she felt. The realization brought a profound sense of relief. She did not want to hate Jonas. What she felt for Jonas was much more complex: part wariness, part grief . . . part longing. She looked across the desktop at Davis, who was eyeing her curiously. How could she explain such a thing to him? She hardly understood it herself.

"Oh, I don't know," she said dismissively. "Hate's a strong word. Let's just say I wish they'd keep to their end of the business world and stay away from mine."

"And which end is that?" Davis baited her.

Catherine grinned. "Why, the successful end, of course!

What did you think I meant, Davis?" She folded her arms behind her head and leaned against the high back of her expensive leather chair. "In just a little more than two days, we're going to put the final nail in the coffin. We're going to clinch this deal, and we're going to be the next advertising firm to lead an American shoe corporation to greatness."

She tried to sound enthusiastic. Positive thinking, she reminded herself, led to positive results. She had every reason to be excited, after all. The presentation had gone well. Leo clearly liked them . . . or at least he'd liked Daphne. Things hadn't gone exactly according to plan, but they had somehow snagged the pole position, and she was determined to keep it. If they got this account, Salinger & Associates would be set for the next four years, if not for the rest of her life. It was the opportunity she had fantasized about since she began her career. All of her dreams were about to come true.

At least, that's what she told herself. But this time, Cat's inner pep talk failed to cheer her. And for the first time in many years, she found it was getting harder and harder to remember exactly what mattered most.

The fresh, barely acrid scent of freshly cut meadow flowers filled Catherine's nostrils from the enormous bouquet she carried in her arms. Her eyes surveyed the crazy assortment: black-eyed Susans, dahlias, sunflowers, daisies . . . all of Daphne's favorites. To an outsider, there was no apparent rhyme or reason to the selection. But Catherine remembered how, during her early years, Daphne had spent countless hours in the flower garden behind their Hollywood Hills home. This grouping reflected Daphne's most favored childhood friends.

Every Thursday after the gardener would come, Cat remembered fondly, scraps of blossoms and leaves would appear in the bin reserved for yard debris. Though the bits of root and stem quickly rotted in the hot Los Angeles sun, Daphne would climb into the bin—no matter how many times she was scolded—and make poor-man's daisy chains out of the clippings the gardener left. When Cat asked her why she didn't just pick the best flowers for her craft work, Daphne stubbornly refused to "kill" the living plants. Even when Cat explained that the flowers were only *part* of the plants and that the growths would survive a small child's bit of pruning, Daphne insisted upon playing with her floral castoffs.

Catherine surveyed the cluster she now held. She was glad she'd taken an early break and gone out to buy the gift for her sister. But somehow, the bouquet didn't look exactly right. The flowers looked too . . . fresh. She grinned. Perhaps she should take them out of their water and leave them in the hot summer sun for a while before presenting them to her sister. Daphne would get a good chuckle from that. At least, Cat thought she would. She didn't really know for sure; it had been so long since the two of them had laughed together.

Lucy's words from the Wednesday before had been on her mind all week. And maybe Lucy was right. Maybe she *had* been a bit hard on Daphne, especially about the Apollo deal. Daphne's intentions had been good. She had thought she was helping, and in fact she *had* improved their standing with the corporation. For goodness' sake, she had single-handedly written the favored ad.

Cat chuckled. So much for letting the consequences teach Daphne a lesson. But still, if she was going to be mature, she would have to admit that things had all worked out for the best. This time around, there was nothing to do but let Daphne feel good about the admittedly bizarre, but nevertheless genuine, contribution she had made.

Most important of all, Leo was clearly impressed with

Daphne. Despite Cat's concerns, Daphne would have to be involved in the next phase of negotiations. The decision was out of Catherine's hands: Leo wanted Daph there. End of story. And if Daphne was going to be there, it was time for Catherine to make peace. Time to swallow her pride. Time to thank Daphne for all the hard work she had put into the Apollo bid.

Catherine paused outside of Daphne's office. Her hands were damp from holding the flowers . . . or was that simply due to a case of nerves? She had no idea where to begin.

Hi, Daph? Are you still mad at me? Too wimpy.

Look, Daphne, I think this has gone on long enough. I don't want to fight anymore, and I don't think you do either. So I say we just put this behind us. Nah. Too bossy.

Hey, Daphne! How are you doing? Ooh, you look great today. Where'd you get that blouse? That's a great color on you. Too weaselly.

"Oh, brother!" Catherine finally gave up rehearsing and decided to just walk in and speak off the cuff. Taking a deep breath, she stepped into her sister's office and saw . . .

Nothing.

Well, that was a lot of buildup for something that didn't even happen. Catherine felt a bit embarrassed. Probably she was just blowing this whole situation up into something larger than what it really was. She and Daphne didn't really have any serious communication problems. That was just an exaggeration on Lucy's part.

She thought back to the previous week's dinner, which she, Lucy, and Felicia had eaten at a small Mexican restaurant on the Pacific Coast Highway. When Lucy went to visit the restroom, Catherine had seized the opportunity to question her other sister.

"Fee?" she asked as her closest sibling dug into a huge

mound of Spanish rice. "Do you think I'm too hard on Daphne?"

"Do you *see* this stuff?" Felicia asked as she picked at the sticky mass with a fork. As a wife and mother of two, she had done her fair share of cooking and had little patience for poorly prepared food. "You could hang *wallpaper* with this stuff. It's like glue!"

"Fee?" Cat tried again, nudging her sister's elbow.

"What?" Felicia looked up from her science project. "Oh. You and Daphne? I dunno. I hardly see you together. You get along well enough, I suppose. Is that what you mean?"

Catherine looked at her thoughtfully. "I'm not sure. I suppose so."

Now, in retrospect, she didn't know whether to cling to Felicia's words as comfort or to discount them because of their source. After all, when it came to relationships, Felicia wasn't doing so well either. Although her husband, Robert, had been considered a very good catch when she married him ten years ago, he had proven to be a difficult man to live with, and these days Felicia was not always sure she was up to the challenge. Exacting and critical by nature, Robert had been less than patient with Felicia for not losing all the weight she'd gained after the birth of their second child, Clifford. Worst of all, Felicia was beginning to suspect that other women still considered her husband 'a catch' . . . and that perhaps he agreed with them.

No, Felicia could hardly be counted on to define a healthy relationship. It had been years since she'd actually been a part of one.

Catherine sighed and looked at the bunch of flowers in her hand. Well, there was no point in letting them dry out, no matter what Daphne's childhood experience had been. She quickly made her way down to the company kitchenette, where she found a tall, cheap-looking vase that had been abandoned by one of her employees after a previous birthday or Valentine's Day.

She filled the vase with water, arranged the flowers to the best of her ability, then left them in the middle of Daphne's desk. When she returned to her own office, neither Robin nor the temp—Carol?—was anywhere to be seen. But on the corner of Cat's desk lay an envelope that had obviously been delivered by special courier. Ripping open the outer envelope, she pulled out a smaller pink one that was addressed with just one word:

Cat.

Catherine's hands began to shake slightly. Why would anyone send a personal note—if it was addressed to "Cat," that's what it had to be—by courier? Something felt wrong . . . very wrong.

She rolled her high-backed chair away from the desk and slowly lowered herself onto it. With trembling fingers, she tore open the envelope and carefully read the letter she found within, written in Daphne's loopy script:

Dear Cat,

It would be silly to say, "Please don't be mad at me." I know you already are—and what I'm doing now is going to upset you even more. Please know that I never wanted to make you angry. That's never been my goal. I just want to be me, to live my own life. That's all. I know you think I'm flaky. And maybe I am. Maybe that's why I'm doing this—who knows? But whatever the reason, this is my decision. I'm making it for me. This is not about you, okay? Don't take it personally. And don't try to stop me.

My goodness, that sounded very dramatic! Stop me from what? Don't worry, I'm not doing anything dangerous. I'm just getting married. "Just" getting married. Doesn't that sound funny? Well, maybe it doesn't to you right now, but I got a little laugh out of it. I know I haven't even told you I was dating anyone, but I have been—for three months now. And I'm completely and totally in love. You'd really like him . . . if you let yourself get to know him. But I know you won't do that. Not now. Not the way things are. That's why we're eloping. There's no way you'd accept Elliott as my boyfriend. But you'll have to accept him, won't you, after he's my husband? At least, that's what I hope.

As you may have guessed by now, the man I love is Elliott Riley. Now, don't spaz out, Cat. He's not the bad guy you think he is. He's sweet and kind, and he loves me very, very much. You'll see. We'll be married soon, and then we'll come home and work everything out. I know this must upset you right now, but in the long run I think you'll see that this is good for both of us. I'm getting married—growing up, like you've been saying for years that I should do. And you are going to learn that I *can* make decisions for myself. I can run my own life and not mess it up. Please trust me to do the right thing, Kitty. I'm not the screw-up you think I am.

Please don't give my office to the janitor while I'm gone. (Just kidding!) Tell Felicia I love her. And please don't yell at Lucy. This isn't her fault. If you're going to blame someone, blame me.

I hope I don't cause too much trouble for you, leaving like this. I do have vacation time coming. (I checked it out with Personnel.) And the work's done on the Apollo account, at least for now. And I'd guess that you're not going to let me into their presence again anytime this century, anyway.

And so I guess I'll see you in a week or so . . . when I'm Mrs. Elliott Riley! (Sorry. That wasn't nice of me. Are you off the floor yet?) Seriously, I do love you, sis. I hate doing it this way, because I know it has to be hurting you. But everything will be okay, I promise. Until next week . . .

Your not-so-little sister,
Daphne

Catherine shook her head angrily. *No.* It couldn't be true. This had to be some mistake. It had been an impulse, nothing more—one of Daphne's crazy, harebrained, whimsical plans that would fizzle out long before it had come to fruition.

She would go to Daphne's place . . . that's what she'd do. Perhaps she'd find some clue there that would help. Maybe Daphne was at the beach house right now, packing. Or, better yet, already regretting the foolish fancy that had led her to send a note that could cause her embarrassment for years to come.

Be gentle, Cat, she told herself carefully. *Be calm.* She grabbed the phone and hit the automatic-dial button marked L&D.

Please, please . . . let her answer. She let it ring fourteen times before finally giving up.

The lack of response didn't mean anything. Perhaps she was afraid to answer, assuming that Catherine would be furious over her rash departure.

Well, she would fix that misconception right away. She'd go right over, insist that Daphne open the door, and assure her sister that all was forgiven and forgotten.

The situation wasn't unsalvageable. All she had to do was get Daphne to listen . . .

Rather like getting an elephant to fly, but it was worth a shot.

★ ★ ★ ★ ★

"Are you *sure* she didn't say anything to you? Anything at all?" Cat questioned her hastily summoned employees. At least ten of the writers, designers, and executives Daphne associated with regularly were lined up on one side of her office, looking curiously like a police lineup.

"Not a word," volunteered Teri, one of Daphne's closest confidantes at the company. "I mean, I knew she was dating someone, but I had no idea who it was. Probably she didn't want to say anything because of Saundra," Teri said, referring to a woman from Accounting.

"Saundra? What about Saundra?" Cat demanded.

"Well, you know her little sister went to college with Elliott up in the Bay Area. They dated for a while, and I guess it was sort of an ugly split."

"Ugly? How?" Cat felt her maternal instincts shift into even higher gear.

"I guess he . . . well, he dumped her. The sister never got over it. Saundra thinks he's a real ladies' man, or he would never have let her get away."

Great. A ladies' man. Just what we need. Cat was still considering whether to step in or simply let consequences take their course, as Lucy had suggested, when Davis Pierce cut in. "Maybe it's a trick," he said slowly.

"What do you mean?" A chill crept down Cat's spine. "What kind of trick?"

"You know, to mess up the deal. Daphne disappears. You get distracted. And then what happens to the bid?"

Robin snorted. "Davis, that's ridiculous. No one would go to that much trouble to—" She reached out to grab Cat's arm as she flew past. "Where do you think you're going?"

Cat turned to her with grim-faced determination. "To play Stalin."

★ ★ ★ ★ ★

All the way to Malibu, Catherine turned the contents of the letter over and over in her mind. *I know you think I'm flaky,* Daphne had said. It was true. Cat had said as much to Daphne in the past. But she had never intended to be unkind or to hurt Daphne's feelings. Verbal sparring was just part of the way all four sisters related to one another. It was just part of the game . . . or so she had thought.

"Come on. Come *on,*" she complained loudly into the emptiness of the car. Since Daphne was not there to yell at, she found herself directing her anger to the traffic at large. "Move it!"

How could she do this? How could she lie to me? For three months, Daphne had lived a charade. Even Catherine, who saw her every day, had no idea that she was seeing anyone special. In fact, she'd had the distinct impression that Daphne was sort of playing the field. Although, now that she thought about it, it had probably been several months since she'd bothered even to ask Daphne about her social life. With their father's death and her new responsibilities, the idea of *anybody* dating just hadn't occurred to her.

She wondered if anyone else knew about Daphne and Elliott. Certainly it would have been impossible to keep the truth from *everyone.*

Then Cat paled. *Lucy.* Lucy knew! That's what Daphne meant when she said, "Please don't yell at Lucy. This isn't her fault." That's why she had said, "Tell Felicia I love her" and not "Tell Fee and Lucy I love them." She'd already said good-bye to Lucy, *because Lucy knew everything!*

Slowly the truth began to grow clearer as Catherine turned the clues over and over in her mind: Daphne giving Jonas looks of warning at Apollo Athletics . . . because he knew she was seeing Elliott and she didn't want him to give anything

94

away. Daphne and Lucy both defending the Rileys, trying to get Cat to change her views about them. And Lucy answering vaguely when Catherine asked questions about where Daphne spent her evenings. It was all a cover-up! Wasn't there *anyone* she could trust?

Cat could barely contain her fury. Her mind raced, searching for a scapegoat. It found one: Jonas Riley.

Daphne's behavior was deplorable, but in many ways understandable. She was young, impetuous, and—Catherine turned her eyes heavenward—supposedly in love. Cat was not surprised that her quirky sister had done such a thing.

Even Lucy's actions were somewhat forgivable. Obviously Lucy had been wrong in not telling Cat what was going on, but it must have been a difficult decision. Her loyalties must have been painfully divided. Cat could almost sympathize.

Almost.

But there was no excuse whatsoever that could induce Cat to forgive Jonas Riley for his part in the whole sordid affair. He had to have known what was going on from the very beginning. "It's good to see you . . . again," he had said to Daphne. Had he been laughing at Catherine that day—knowing that he held a secret that, if revealed, would surely break her heart? Just as he had laughed at her and Daphne during the Apollo meeting? Normally composed Catherine felt a stinging sensation behind her eyes and struggled to blink back the tears.

Well, she'd show him! Just as soon as she had this mess with Daphne straightened out, she'd go and give that man a piece of her mind! No one messed with her family and got away with it. No one.

Not even Mr. Jonas Riley.

It didn't take Catherine long to figure out that Daphne

really was gone. Long gone, in fact. She'd given Daph a full thirty seconds to open the door before pulling out her spare key and letting herself into the beach house.

A quick walk-through revealed that no one was home. Several minutes later she had also determined that Daphne's small suitcase was gone. She decided to conduct a methodical search of Daphne's room to ascertain what had been taken. A swimsuit? Ski pants? Sundresses? Hiking boots?

She expected Daphne's closet to be as big a mess as her office, which was chronically littered and disorganized. But as it turned out, her sister's bedroom was nearly as neat as her own . . . and yielded almost no clues as to where its owner had gone. She had no idea where Daphne kept things like her passport or checkbook. And she doubted she would unearth any further clues by searching the house.

Catherine went to the front room to call Lucy at work and Fee at home—getting voice mail for both. After leaving frantic messages on both their systems, she grabbed the telephone book and looked up the name *Riley*. To her dismay, there were several dozen listings for that name, but none for "Elliott," "Miles," or "Jonas." And nothing in the business listings or yellow pages for the Riley Agency.

"It figures they'd be unlisted," she grumbled bitterly. "Probably to keep away the hoards of angry people who want to hunt them down."

It hit her then that the Rileys probably hadn't been in town long enough to obtain a listing. Punching the numbers for Information into the keypad, she waited impatiently for an operator to respond.

"For what city?" the automated attendant queried.

"Los Angeles."

"For what listing?"

"The Riley Agency—right away!"

★ ★ ★ ★ ★

So all-consuming was her anger, Catherine didn't have energy left to worry about her imminent confrontation with Jonas Riley. It did not occur to her that to her competitors—the creative members of the Riley Agency team—she might appear less like a justifiably angry protector of innocents than a certifiably crazy person. It did not even cross her mind that Jonas might see her not as a dangerous force to be reckoned with but rather as a hot-tempered maniac.

Catherine had only one thing on her mind. And she wasn't about to stop until she'd had her say.

By the time she reached the Riley Agency offices, she was practically breathing fire. She stormed into the reception area feeling hot and flushed, and the woman at the front desk looked up at her in alarm. Clearly she feared that Cat would fall on the floor in some kind of seizure or pull out a weapon and start shouting demands. Instead, Cat forced herself to approach the counter slowly and speak in a calm voice.

"Is Jonas Riley in?" she enunciated carefully.

"Uh . . . may I tell him who's asking?" the woman inquired, wide-eyed.

"Yes," said Catherine levelly. "Tell him his conscience is here."

"His conscience. Okay." The receptionist seemed to take this at face value. "Do you have an appointment?" she asked helpfully.

Catherine stared. She could not believe her ears. "No," she said in a voice that betrayed her disbelief. "I really don't. I think he'll see me though."

The woman hesitated, one finger poised above the intercom button. Then she looked up at Cat and said apologetically, "I'm really not supposed to buzz him without a name."

Oh, for goodness' sake. "It's Salinger. Catherine Salinger," she said. "Tell him it's an emergency."

The woman's eyes grew even more saucer-like upon hearing Cat's name. Clearly she knew who the competition was.

"Well . . . actually, I don't know if he's in right now," the receptionist told her, looking around as if for backup. Cat didn't know if the woman had actually summoned someone to "bounce" her, but she couldn't afford to find out. She'd have to call the woman's bluff.

"Then you won't mind if I just take a quick look around to see for myself," she said brightly . . . and ducked into the hallway behind the desk.

"Hey! You can't just—"

Within seconds, Catherine had ditched the woman who had, understandably, seemed reluctant to trail her. For all the receptionist knew, Cat might have been a dangerous, escaped criminal. Besides, who would answer the phones if she walked away? A good receptionist never leaves her post.

Catherine almost smiled at the assessment, which she suspected hit pretty close to the mark. But she had no time to indulge in self-entertainment. She had to find Jonas Riley . . . and fast.

The task turned out to be much easier than she imagined. After poking her head into the offices of an accountant, a graphic designer, and what appeared to be a professional, purple-haired punk rocker, she found herself in an impressive-looking hallway that she suspected would lead to the Riley Agency's executive offices.

Her suspicions proved correct. On a sign in front of the door just ahead, she could make out the words: Jonas Riley. For just a moment she faltered. Then hearing the sound of angry, concerned voices in the hallway behind her, she plunged on ahead, stepping into the office where a silver-haired man bent over some papers on the desk in front of Jonas.

"A-*hem*." She cleared her throat loudly.

Jonas looked up in surprise . . . and his jaw dropped at the sight of her. His expression quickly changed from one of shock to one of . . . amusement?

He stared.

Catherine looked down at herself and, for a moment, saw herself as Jonas saw her—red-faced and rumpled. She'd been running around all morning without a thought to her appearance. Her mint-green silk charmeuse blouse had become partially untucked at the front of her knee-length black skirt. Her hair—she now felt rather than saw—had come loose from the black clip that once had held it back in a smooth, formidable style, leaving wisps of unruly blond hair all about her face. And somewhere along the way, she had managed to sustain a scrape on her knee that was bleeding a little and had caused her sheer black nylons to run all the way down to her toes.

Jonas, in contrast, looked completely put together in dark, loose-fitting slacks and a gray, cable-knit sweater over a white T-shirt. Seeing him, Cat's cheeks burned hotter than ever as she threw him an accusatory glance.

"Cat," he said, grinning, "what on earth happened? You look like a train hit you. Do you want to come in? I was just going over some figures with—"

But before he could get the words out, his companion had turned around, and Catherine saw for herself exactly who Jonas had been going over figures with.

"Miles." The word fell like a stone from her lips.

The man looked confused. He looked first at her, then turned back to his son. "Cat? You don't mean Catherine—?"

"Catherine Salinger?" she supplied helpfully. "As in *Edward Salinger's daughter?* Yes, that's me."

"But—" Now Miles really looked perplexed. "Well, we haven't seen you since—"

"Since you stabbed my father in the back, I believe." She kept her voice low and even.

Miles's eyes darted around the room nervously. "Cat, I'm so sorry about your dad."

"That's not why I'm here."

Silence fell heavily over the room, only to be broken as a small group of angry-looking men and one woman burst inside.

"That's her," the receptionist supplied unnecessarily, as if more than one bleeding, unidentified crazy woman could be found wandering around the building.

"Do you want us to escort her out?" an eager-looking young executive asked Jonas. It took a moment, but Cat eventually recognized him as the man she had seen with Jonas in the Apollo lobby. She cringed inwardly but forced herself to stand tall and proud—or at least, as proud as possible under the circumstances.

"No, that's all right," Jonas said with mock seriousness. He turned and gave Catherine a sly wink. "If Ms. Salinger needs an escort, I'll be happy to do the job."

"Why, I—!"

"Settle down, now, Cat," he laughed. "I didn't mean it that way, and you know it. Although, if you'd like to join me for coffee . . ."

Catherine opened her mouth to speak, found she could not, then drew a deep breath and tried again.

"Believe me, I am not here to get a date from you or anyone else," she said. "Nor did I come to engage in small talk about my father—with either of you." She threw Miles a look of disgust. To her surprise, the man seemed to shrink under her gaze.

Catherine turned back to Jonas. "I came to find out where your brother has taken my sister."

Jonas opened his mouth to respond, but she continued

before he could utter a word. "I know you and your father are behind this. Don't think that I don't."

Jonas looked completely confused. "Sorry?"

"You should be."

"No, I mean . . . I'm afraid I don't know what you're talking about."

Catherine folded her arms across her chest. "Right." She tried to sound tough, but inside she wanted to cry. She wished all those people would leave, including Miles. All she could deal with now was Jonas, and facing off with him was almost more than she could bear. She choked back the tears that threatened to rise.

"Seriously, Cat. I really don't know what you mean." Jonas turned to face the crowd that still gathered at the doorway. "You all can go back to work now. Everything's under control." Reluctantly the group dispersed, leaving Catherine alone with the two Rileys.

"I, uh, think I'll talk a walk myself," Miles suggested. He moved toward the door, but then stopped at Catherine's side. "I know you're angry with me, but I really am sorry about your dad. Really, I am. He was a good man."

His words surprised her. Catherine looked up at Miles, her face frozen with shock. "That's right," she said finally and watched him go.

Then she was alone with Jonas.

With slow movements, as one approaching an animal in the wild, he stepped over to her, took her trembling hands in his, and led her to a chair.

"There, now," he said soothingly. "Isn't that better? Now why don't you tell me what this is all about? Why do you think your sister has disappeared? And why on earth would you think I had anything to do with it?"

Cat pulled her hand away. "Don't be patronizing. I don't

want to fight. I just want to find Daphne. I know you know where she is."

"And how do you know that?" Jonas asked gently.

"Because I'm sure you're in on it. Look, Jonas, I don't care. Really. It was a good trick. But now it's over. If you'll just tell me—"

Jonas was beginning to look angry. "What do you mean, a good trick?"

Catherine had been averting her eyes, trying to avoid his gaze. But now she forced herself to look at him directly and tell him what she knew.

"I know that you and your father will do anything to get an account. It's always been that way, ever since your dad and mine split up. But this is my sister we're talking about."

He just looked at her, his face unreadable. A bit unnerved, but determined, she plunged on: "You must have noticed how much Leo and the others liked Daphne. So now you've gotten her out of town, and that could very well ruin our meeting on Friday. Very clever. Well done, I suppose, if you admire that sort of thing. But I don't care about the ad campaign, okay? Not as much as I care about my sister. Apparently she really thinks your brother is in love with her. And when she finds out this is all a trick to get information out of her or to force her to mess up the bid, it's going to break her heart. Doesn't that mean anything to you, Jonas?" she asked desperately. Wasn't there even a shadow left of the man she had once loved? "Don't you care about Daphne at all?"

Throughout her speech, Jonas had listened silently. But with each word, his features had settled into a deepening mask of anger. "Is that really what you think of me?"

Cat shook her head. "Jonas, this isn't about you. It doesn't matter what I think of—"

"It matters to me," he said dully. "It matters a lot." He

rose from the chair he had pulled up beside her and began to pace the room. For several long minutes he walked, back and forth, without speaking. The silence was maddening to Catherine, but somehow she could not bring herself to break it. At last he spoke.

"You know, Cat," he said, turning away from the sun-streaked window. "Ever since I saw you the other day, I've been thinking about you. Thinking about the way things used to be, about how I wish you didn't see me as an enemy. I've always cared about you, Cat, more than you ever realized. More than you ever could believe." His voice broke, and he turned back to the window and stared outside.

"But you obviously think I'm a monster. So I guess that's all there is to say about that. If your opinion of me is that low, what else can I do? Force you to go out to dinner with me? Insist that you give me another chance? That's sort of ridiculous, isn't it?" He scratched his strong chin and laughed a humorless laugh.

"You clearly think me incapable of such human emotions as compassion and love. And that's fine. Think what you want about me." He turned back to her and spoke earnestly. "But my brother, Elliott, is a good person. He cares deeply for Daphne. Now, I don't agree that eloping is necessarily a wise choice—yes, I know they've run off together—but I do believe the decision is theirs to make." His eyes begged her to understand.

"Try to give them the benefit of the doubt, Cat. They're two young people in love—and they're not teenagers anymore. Elliott's twenty-five years old. What's Daphne, twenty-three, twenty-four? They know what they're doing, at least as much as anyone does. They've got their priorities straight. They love God. They love each other. What else is there?"

He stepped back to her side, knelt, and took her hands once again. "What else *could* there be? Love is love, Cat. It's a powerful thing. It's a force that stirs people, that changes hearts—changes lives." He looked at her thoughtfully. "You should give it a try." The words were barely more than a whisper, but they echoed loudly in Catherine's heart. She stood abruptly and pulled her hands away.

"Where'd they go, Jonas?" she said, working hard to keep all emotion from her voice. "You have to tell me where they went so I can do something about this."

"Sorry." Jonas shook his head. "I'm on love's side." The look he gave her was one of disappointment. "You should be too."

"Augh!" Catherine cried in frustration. "Well, I'll find them anyway. I'm going to stop this wedding if it's the last thing I do."

His soft brown eyes looked at her in surprise, then hardened as he said simply: "Not if I have anything to say about it."

"Well, this time, Mr. Riley . . . you won't."

Without another word, Catherine spun on her heel, haughtily lifted her chin . . . and, to her great embarrassment, made a decidedly undramatic exit as her bloody knee stiffened up and she was forced to hobble all the way out the door.

Six

"Think, Fee. *Think*," Catherine pleaded. Eagerly she leaned forward from her perch on one of the blue-and-white-striped, slipcovered couches in Felicia's sunlit sitting room. "Didn't Daphne say *anything* to you about who she was seeing or what she was planning?"

Felicia shook her head, making her long, dark hair swing. "I've barely even spoken to her in the last two weeks. She didn't show up at dinner last Wednesday, remember? And before that, I think it had been several days since I even talked to her on the phone. Honey, what *is* it?" This last comment she directed at her eight-year-old daughter, Dinah, who stood beside her, plucking at her sleeve. "Mommy's talking to Aunt Cat."

Dinah looked at her mother with wide, serious gray eyes—the one physical trait she had obviously inherited from her father. "Mommy," she said quietly. "Is Auntie Daphne okay?"

"Sweetheart!" Felicia scooped up the grave little child and pulled her into her lap. "Aunt Daphne is fine," she said, patting her daughter comfortingly on the back. "She just went on a little trip, that's all, and Auntie Cat wants to find her."

Cat bristled. "So do you. Don't you, Fee?"

"What?" Felicia stared out the sitting room doorway, distracted by a banging noise that was emerging from one of the bedrooms at the end of the hall. "Clifford?" she called to her five-year-old. "What are you doing down there?"

105

The banging stopped.

"Nothing," an innocent-sounding voice lilted back.

"Fee?"

"Hmm?" Cat's voice drew Felicia's attention back to the issue at hand. "Oh, yes. Of course. I agree with you," she said absently, and began to fiddle with her daughter's long, soft plaits of hair.

"Oh?" Cat looked at her skeptically. "And what exactly did I say that you agree with?"

"That . . . we should call in the FBI? I don't know, Cat," she sighed and dropped Dinah's braid from her hand. "Look, I know you're worried. I am too. What Daphne's doing is . . . well, rash. But I don't see what we can do about it."

"We can find her," Cat said resolutely. "We *will* find her. We'll track down her irresponsible hide and drag that girl back home."

Felicia blinked at her, shocked by the coarseness of Cat's words and tone. "And if she doesn't want to come home?"

Cat fell back against the soft cushions and looked at her sister despairingly. "You don't think I can convince her?"

"That's not what I said," Fee told her. "I said she may not want to come home. You may *get* her to do it. But in that case, I don't think what Daphne *wants* is the issue."

"So you're saying you think I'd be forcing her?" Catherine suddenly felt very lonely. She really *was* perceived as an ogre. How long had her sisters felt this way about her?

"No," Fee said in a calm, cool voice. "I'm just saying that you can be very . . . convincing. You're more strong-willed even than Daphne. When it comes to battles, I daresay you'll always win. Maybe that's why she doesn't fight fair. She hasn't got a chance in an even match. So she has to pull tricks on you, like she did on the day of your big meeting. Or she has to run off. It's the only way she can beat you. Although, in this case, I don't think beating *you* is the issue so much as winning for herself."

Catherine thought about this. "You're saying that when we have a conflict, I make her choose between what she wants and what I want? And that because I always win, she's been forced to run away in order to take care of herself?"

Felicia turned her palms upward, refusing to get involved more deeply than she already was. "That's your interpretation, Cat. Only you and Daphne know the dynamics of your relationship. Anything else—from any*one* else—is a matter of speculation. That includes anything Lucy or I say—or even Jonas Riley."

The look Cat gave her was sharp. "What do you know about what Jonas said?"

"Only what you told me." Fee looked at her knowingly. "And that's not much. But I can tell that whatever it was, it really bothered you."

Cat turned away. She was tired of being psychoanalyzed by her sisters. "What is it with you and Lucy these days? What makes you so sure Jonas Riley has such an impact on me all of a sudden? He's just an former acquaintance. An irritating, dishonest, meddling former acquaintance."

"There's nothing sudden about what we think." Felicia said simply. "The only thing sudden is the fact that you've run into him again after all these years. He's always had this sort of effect on you—and you've always cared what he thought. I think Jonas's opinion once meant more to you than anyone's. Maybe it still does."

Cat snorted. "Please. That's ridiculous."

"Oh. Sorry." Felicia grinned and faked her own piglike snort of laughter.

Despite herself, Catherine felt a smile tug at her lips. "Stop that!"

Fee's grin softened into a look of sympathy. "There's a girl," she said encouragingly. "That's the first smile I've seen on you all day." She patted the bottom of the demure eight-year-old she still held in her lap. "Go on, Dinah. I think Auntie Cat needs a hug before she gets on her way." Her faced crinkled up, making her dark eyebrows meet over her finely arched nose.

"I think she's going to need it."

Catherine's cell phone finally rang shortly after she had made it back to her home near USC.

"Lucy!" she cried, flopping down onto her antique black-walnut bed. "Thank *goodness* it's you. Where have you been? I've been calling you all day!"

"So I heard," Lucy remarked. Her voice sounded guarded. "I was at a meeting for professional businesswomen in downtown L.A. We met to—"

"Sorry," Cat broke in. "I don't really care about that right now. I just want to know: *Where is our sister?*"

"Um . . . which one?" Lucy sounded incredibly guilty. She was terrible at playing dumb.

"Nice try, but don't expect an Academy Award anytime soon. You know very well which sister I mean. *Where is Daphne, Luce?*"

The telephone earpiece filled with static caused by a dramatic sigh. "I don't know, Cat. I really don't. Daphne wouldn't tell me *where* she was going 'cause she knew you'd get it out of me. All she told me was *what* she was doing. I tried to talk her out of it, I swear. But once she had her mind made up, there was no stopping her."

"No stopping her? *No stopping her?*" Cat grumbled. "*I* could have stopped her!"

"Maybe," Lucy agreed. "But she didn't want to be stopped."

Catherine held the phone out in front of her and stared at it. Was this conversation really happening? She put the mouthpiece back to her lips. "Are you *sure* you don't know where she went?"

"I'm sure."

"*Completely* sure?"

"Scout's honor."

Catherine pursed her lips primly. "You were never a Scout."

"I was a Bluebird."

"Not the same thing."

"Is that my fault?" Lucy said easily. "Guess you'll just have to take my word for it."

"All right then." Catherine took a deep breath. "If you don't know where she is, tell me everything you *do* know. And I mean *everything*. Don't leave out a single detail." She fingered the soft, worn fabric of the quilt upon which she lay, tracing with her fingers the cream and celery-green squares that made up the old-fashioned pattern.

"Well, I guess Daphne ran into Elliott several months ago, at some art show downtown. They went out together for coffee that night, and Daphne said they stayed at the restaurant until really late, just talking."

"Just talking," Cat grumbled. "Didn't she care that his father was the one who caused Daddy so much misery?"

For several moments, only silence greeted her. Then Lucy offered, "You know, Cat, it wasn't just Miles who hurt Daddy. I know he had a hard life, but you can't blame it all on the Rileys. Mother's death hurt him, too—and all the financial problems they had at Salinger & Riley."

"But they were very successful!" Catherine protested.

"Creatively, yes," Lucy agreed. "But you know as well as anybody that Daddy wasn't all that great about handling the money. And back then, he insisted that he be the one to make the major financial decisions. He'd majored in business in college, and he figured he was the one with the best training. But his gifts were in the area of creativity, not in finance or management. Miles was the natural businessman. He still is. That's why he started trying to get his own clients."

Catherine listened, horrified by what she was hearing, even though it rang true in the back of her mind. "Who told you all this?"

"Daphne," Lucy admitted.

"And I suppose she heard it from Elliott? Or maybe even Miles himself?"

"I guess so. I'm not really sure which one." For a moment, even Lucy sounded a bit unsure of what to think.

"Don't you get it, Lucy? That's what they *wanted* Daphne and the rest of us to believe. They're trying to put the blame on Daddy, because Miles certainly doesn't want to shoulder it."

"Now, I don't think that's true," Lucy protested. "Daphne said that Miles was really sorry about everything that happened between them. He realized that he let business get in the way of friendship, and he admitted that he had done some really rotten things."

"If that's true, then why didn't he ever apologize to Daddy?"

"I don't know," Lucy said helplessly. "How do we know he never did? Daphne seemed to think he had."

That, Catherine could not accept. "No. I don't think so. If anything like that had happened, Daddy would have told us. He would have said something." At least, she thought he would. Unless he blamed himself for what happened between her and Jonas. Or thought she wouldn't understand. Or meant to tell her . . . and never had time . . .

This new line of thinking unnerved her a bit, but she was unwilling to consider it further at the moment. "Whatever," she said impatiently. "So Daphne ran into Elliott, and they stayed up at the restaurant talking half the night. After that, I presume, they started dating?"

"Did they ever!" Lucy whistled long and low. "I swear, those two were practically joined at the hip. They went everywhere together. They were like a couple of teenagers."

"Hmph," Cat grunted. "That sounds healthy." Her voice was dripping with sarcasm. "Haven't they ever heard of personal space? Boundaries?"

"Listen to you, *Dr.* Salinger!" Lucy laughed. "Be a sport. They're young and in love."

"Yes, they are," Cat agreed. "*Young* being the operative word. And so then what?"

"Well, in the last month or so, they started spending even more time together, if that's possible. If Daphne wasn't at home sleeping or at the office working on the Apollo bid, she was with Elliott."

"And you knew about it the whole time."

"Yep."

"But you didn't tell me about it?"

"Nope."

Catherine grabbed the telephone in a choke hold and throttled it, then lifted the receiver back to her lips and asked in a calm voice. "And why not?"

"Because Daphne asked me not to," Lucy said simply. "She said she'd tell you in her own time, when it was right. She knew you were all whacked out about the Rileys, and she thought maybe she could change your mind about them before she broke the news."

Cat thought about the conversation she'd had with

Daphne in the lobby at Apollo Athletics. "That sounds about right. She brought the subject up just last week."

"And what happened?" Lucy feigned innocence, but Catherine got the feeling she already knew.

"I . . . I didn't listen," she admitted. "I was going to talk to her about it later, but then Jonas Riley came in and I sort of came unglued."

"Went a bit bonkers on her, did you?"

"Mmm. A bit," Cat admitted.

"Yeah, that's what she said. I think that's when she decided to run off with Elliott. She knew you'd never listen to her under the circumstances . . . so she decided to change the circumstances."

"But . . . but that's insane!" Catherine protested.

"Perhaps. But consider who we're talking about here. Have crazy ideas ever stopped Daphne before?"

"What did you say to her?"

"Pretty much the same things you've been saying to me. Except I did a lot less shrieking."

"So . . . what more can you tell me?"

"Nothing."

"I see." Catherine tried to think of another approach. "You're not going to volunteer any more information?"

"Nope. Honest, Cat, I was sworn to secrecy."

"Can I ask you twenty questions?" she tried. Her sisters were lunatics, but she knew what made them tick.

"Well . . ." Lucy sounded reluctant, but at least she didn't refuse.

Catherine felt a glint of hope. "Do you know where Daphne went?"

"No I don't."

Cat stewed about this.

"Seriously," Lucy told her, as if she could read Cat's

expression from over the phone. "I really don't. But keep trying."

"Do you know when she left?"

"Mmm . . . yes."

Catherine waited, then cried impatiently, "Well, when *was* it?"

"Sorry," Lucy said wickedly. "I'm only accepting yes and no questions."

Catherine took a deep breath and counted to ten while envisioning appropriate punishments she would inflict upon her sister when this whole sorry mess was over. "Was it this weekend?" she said evenly.

"No."

"Today?"

"No."

"Last week?"

"Uh—."

"Was it—? Oh, no. When did I see her last—Monday? She didn't leave on *Tuesday,* did she?"

Lucy paused, then finally said, "Yes."

Cat sat up on the bed and gripped the phone more firmly. *Now* they were getting somewhere.

"Oh *nooooooooooo,*" Cat cried.

"What's the matter?"

"That's been *days,*" she said helplessly. "They must be married by now."

Lucy responded with only silence.

"I said, 'They must be married by now,' " Catherine repeated. "Right, Lucy?"

Nothing.

"Right, Lucy?"

A slight pause. Then, quietly: "Not necessarily."

Catherine sat up straight on the bed. "You *know* something. Don't deny it. You may not know where they're getting married, but you know when it's happening. *Don't* you?"

"Is that one of your twenty questions?"

"*When* are they getting married?"

Lucy sighed. "On Friday."

"Friday? Friday! That gives us more than three full days to find them."

"Gives *you* three full days to find them—*if* you can. Anyway, I *think* it's Friday. Unless they change their minds."

"You're a glass-is-half-empty sort of gal, aren't you?" Cat said dryly. "Don't rain on my parade. This means we've actually got a chance!"

"I think you're in the wrong line of work. You ought to be a motivational speaker."

"Thanks. Since you think so, why don't you motivate yourself right on over here and help me do a little detective work?"

"Oh, Cat, I can't," Lucy protested. "I've got meetings all afternoon. It's just too late to break them."

"Lucy," Cat said in her most threatening voice.

"Oh, all right. I tell you what: I'll have my secretary reschedule everything I've got planned for tomorrow. But that's the best I can do. If you need someone today, why don't you call Fee?"

"She's busy with the kids this afternoon. She said she couldn't help till tomorrow either. But that's okay. I'll manage." Catherine raised herself off the bed, tucked her green silk shirt evenly into her black skirt, and walked over to her dresser to get a new pair of stockings. "Won't you be surprised when I bring those two back tonight from . . . well, from wherever they've gone?"

"Mmm. You go, Cat," Lucy said in an obvious effort to sound supportive. "And . . . Cat?"

"Yes?" Catherine was barely listening now. With her chin

she held the phone in place while using her hands to slip on the fresh stockings. Her thoughts were on the plan that was developing in her head.

"There's one other thing you should know." Suddenly, Lucy sounded very tired. "I guess."

"What is it?" She had Cat's full attention.

"I think there's a chance that Daphne's not . . . really sure," Lucy said quietly. "I trust her to make the right decision ultimately. I really do . . . whatever that is. And she was really excited when she left. But she seemed a bit sad when she called the other day. I tried to talk to her about it, but by then the ball was rolling. I don't think she was willing even to *consider* stopping it." Catherine pondered this new revelation. "I'm pretty sure telling you was the right thing to do," Lucy told her soberly.

"Thanks, Luce." For the first time throughout the ordeal, Catherine felt genuinely grateful for her sister's help. "I'd better go now. Call me if you remember anything else?"

"I will."

And despite the differences of opinion that had come before, Catherine knew without a doubt that Lucy would.

As she made her way down the hall toward Daphne's office, Catherine threw a guilty smile in the direction of each employee she passed. Though the feeling defied all reason, she could not help but suspect they all knew what she was up to.

Catherine Salinger was about to burglarize her sister's office. Her mission: To steal the yellow legal tablet upon which Daphne had been writing her notes for the past several weeks.

It was on this pad that Daphne had scribbled each thought as it came to her concerning the Apollo campaign. One day, as the two of them were discussing the upcoming presentation, Cat had peered over Daphne's shoulder to take a look at some of the notes she'd been taking, and Daphne had hastily pulled the tablet away. At the time, Catherine had dismissed the action as the behavior of a temperamental creative type. In retrospect, she could not help but wonder what Daphne had been so determined not to let her see.

Upon entering the office, Catherine made a beeline for the chronic mess that was Daphne's desk. The flowers now forgotten, she focused entirely on the enormous piles of loose papers that filled every inch of usable space. Earnestly, she searched for any clue that could help her make sense of the situation. If Daphne was getting married on Friday, why had she already disappeared? More important, where was she now?

Though she did not find answers to any of those questions, Catherine was delighted to find the yellow notepad. Most of the notes, punctuated per Daphne's habit with elaborate doodles, were clearly in reference to the Apollo campaign. But on the eighth page, between a bouquet of curving lines and a cartoon cat, Catherine found a cryptic note that immediately drew her eye: *Southern California Charters.*

Cat quickly reached for Daphne's phone and began to dial. Seconds later, Directory Assistance had once again come to her aid. After punching a second set of numbers into the keypad, she heard a scratchy voice answer, "So-Cal Charters."

"Um, hello," she began nervously. "I'm wondering if you can help me. You see, my sister has eloped. And I think you may have talked to her, either about a wedding or a honeymoon trip."

"Could be," the man said reasonably. "I talk to a lot o' folks about stuff like that."

Catherine breathed a deep sigh of relief. She was on their trail at last! "Oh, good. Her name is—"

"Don't matter what her name is," the man interrupted in the same casual tone with which he had answered the line. "I can't really tell ya if I seen her."

"What?" Catherine blinked at the phone in her hand, as if the object itself was being unreasonable. "I'm sorry, I don't understand."

"People come t' me with their private business," he drawled. "And I can't just go sharing that with any ol' stranger that happens t' call and say she's a gal's sister . . ."

"But I assure you," Cat said through clenched teeth, "I *am* her sister. If you would just let me explain—"

"Don't need no explanations," he informed her. "Whether yer her sister or not, and whatever she's done—now, that's *her* private business. I'm afraid I just can't help ya there. So I'll just say 'bye, now. Thanks fer calling." And with that, Catherine found herself listening to the empty drone of a dull dial tone.

"Why, he . . . of all the stubborn—" She stared at the receiver in her hand. What she wanted more than anything was to call back and give the man a piece of her mind. But . . .

Don't do it, Cat, she warned herself. *There's a better way. Remember, victory is the best revenge.*

She stepped over to Daphne's bookcase, where she eventually found a battered phone book tucked between an enormous volume entitled *Advertising Strategies*—apparently a souvenir from Daphne's college days—and a copy of Dr. Seuss's *Horton Hears a Who*. Flipping through the pages, Cat quickly found the address she was searching for—on Balboa Pier.

She grinned a grin of triumph. *Okay, Mr. Southern Cali-*

fornia Charters. I've got you now. Today, you have met your match. I'm about to find out exactly what I want.

And you won't even know what hit you.

SEVEN

"I'm a bride. I'm a bride," Catherine mumbled under her breath. "All I have to do is make this joker think I'm a bride." If the owner of Southern California Charters didn't want to give her any information over the phone, that was just fine with her. She'd simply go to him as a potential client. Perhaps if he was convinced that she was scoping out his services because she herself was going to get married—and someday, she probably would, Cat rationalized—he'd be much more willing to talk. And *that* was when she'd go in for the kill.

"I'm a bride . . . I'm a bride," she continued to mumble as she walked along the pier.

"Oh. Um . . . congratulations," responded a confused-looking man as he passed in the opposite direction. Self-consciously, Catherine returned the man's timid smile and silently vowed that in the future she would keep her self-talks to a whisper.

She had gone over her plan during every moment of the drive from downtown L.A. to Newport Beach. Her approach was simple: She would concoct a story similar to the one Daphne must have given. Cat would tell the man that she planned to have a small, private ceremony and that she was also thinking about taking a brief honeymoon on a sailboat or yacht. Then she'd ask him if any other couples had recently planned the same thing.

It was the perfect plot.

Catherine beamed.

She was actually going to find Daphne and Elliott. And nothing in the world was going to stand in the way of her bringing the two young rebels home.

It was nearly five o'clock by the time she reached the offices of Southern California Charters. Casually she strode in the front door and took a quick survey of her surroundings.

Though the building was situated in Newport Beach's high-rent district, its interior resembled the inside of a poorly maintained real-estate office. The walls were a sterile white, the furniture cheap-looking, and the counters strewn with flyers. On one wall, someone had tacked up pictures of the product the company had to offer: not properties, but over twenty different boats that could be chartered.

Sitting at the far end of the room was a wiry man in his early sixties: five foot six, approximately one hundred forty pounds, wearing a faded blue T-shirt, jeans, and battered sandals, which were now propped up on the Formica desktop in front of him. His face was dark and leathery, giving him the appearance of being a man who loved the ocean and made his living off it. At the moment, he looked slightly tired—as though he had already spent several hours that day at sea.

Cat presumed the slight man to be the individual she had spoken with on the phone. Certainly the scratchy voice sounded the same. She eyed him warily, then pushed her irritation away and, with semidetached interest, listened as he gave his telephone sales spiel to a potential customer.

"Yeah, that's right. We charter off the coast o' Newport year-round. Our full season's June 1 through September 30. Off season's the rest o' the year. We offer real good deals then if ya can't go now." He listened as the client asked another question. Noticing Catherine, he waved to her and held up one aged, weatherworn finger, as if to tell her he would be off the phone momentarily.

"Weekly charters is six full days and nights," he was saying. "During the full season, like it is now, we leave on a Saturday or a Sunday afternoon, comin' back the next Friday or Saturday. There's some midweek departures, too, but ya gotta ask special about those if ya want 'em. They ain't always available. On thirty-foot vessels an' up, we ask fer a three-day reservation, mi-ni-*mum*. I got a business t' run here." He laughed heartily at his own cleverness.

"Nope, nope. Insurance is included. Some o' those other guys'll tack it on extra. But Big Jack won't steer ya wrong."

Big Jack? Catherine swallowed her laughter and raised a brochure to her face to hide her amusement.

The little man held the cream-colored telephone tight against his ear. "Mmm-hm. That's big savings. You betcha. All right then. You come on down and take a look. Give us a call first, make sure we're here. Maybe we'll even take ya out on the water fer a spell. Give ya an idea what yer getting, 'cause we're the best, ya know. I wouldn't lie t' ya."

Poor Daphne, Catherine thought to herself. *I wonder if she fell for his spiel? Come to think of it, she's just as goofy as he is. They'd probably be soul mates . . .*

"Kin I help you?"

Startled, Catherine nearly the dropped her brochure. Suddenly she felt like a very obvious fake.

"Why, yes," she said, then stopped. *Oh, no! What if he recognizes my voice from the telephone?* She had determined that she didn't want to actually lie as part of her investigation. But it seemed only reasonable that she should disguise her voice slightly. "I'm, um—" she began in a slightly lower timbre, "—interested in finding out about the services you offer for weddings and honeymoons."

"Well, now." Big Jack scratched his small chin, which was covered in black stubble flecked with gray and white. "We don't do a lot o' weddin's. It'd have t' be a pretty little one fer that t' work. Our boats aren't all *that* big. What yer prob'ly lookin' fer is a place for yer honey-moon." He looked at her curiously. "Where's yer *fee*-on-*say?* I don't like havin' ta repeat m'self."

"He's . . . not here," Cat said truthfully. *Assuming I won't be marrying Big Jack someday.* "I'm just doing some research about . . . options. Actually, it could very well be just the two of us at the ceremony, along with the minister who will marry us and whoever captains the ship and maybe a witness or two." Catherine swallowed hard. *Who knows?* she told her guilty conscience. *It might turn out just that way someday.*

Carefully she prepared to drop her bomb. "I suppose you *can* do a wedding that way? On one of your boats, I mean? Has anyone else ever planned something like that?"

"Well, sure," Big Jack said unhelpfully, kicking his feet down off the desk. "Whatever you want. We aim t' please. Come on over here, and I'll show ya what we got."

He led her to a side door and walked her down to the docks, where hundreds of boats were moored. "You see that one there?" He pointed toward a small red-and-white vessel that was anchored nearby. "That's the *Mighty Mouse*. She's thirty feet of pure beauty. Engine's twenty-five horsepower, universal diesel. And she sleeps six—" He stopped at the sight of a man approaching from down the pier. "Why, look-y there," he said as the man waved at them. He beamed. "Looks like yer sweetheart done showed up after all."

Catherine turned, not understanding . . . and drew in her breath at the sight of Jonas Riley, who was now less than twenty feet away. No longer within the temperature-controlled atmosphere of his office, Jonas had shed his light gray sweater, leaving only a white T-shirt tucked into his casual slacks. Without thinking, Catherine reached up to smooth her sleek chignon, which she had carefully restyled before driving out to the waterfront. Her silk blouse clung to her skin as, underneath the warm afternoon sun, she felt herself begin to perspire.

Phooey, she thought, squinting at Jonas in irritation. *He's going to give away everything!* "Oh, that's not—" she began to protest, but Big Jack was already reaching out to shake Jonas's hand.

"Well, hello there, young fella!" he said cheerfully. "M' name's Big Jack. Yer missus-to-be an' I was just talkin' about yer weddin' plans."

Jonas nearly choked on the greeting that had formed on his lips. "My . . . missus-to-be?" He looked at Big Jack with questions written all over his face.

In her desperation, Catherine panicked. She stepped forward, reached out and slipped her arm under Jonas's, and smiled up at his face. "Don't say a word, Jonas *dear,*" she said in a sweet, low voice, but her eyes held a warning. "This nice man was just about to tell us some very important information about his boats. And you know how unhappy I get when I miss out on *important information.*"

Jonas looked carefully first at Catherine, then at Jack, then back at the woman now reluctantly masquerading as his fiancée. "Well, then," he said with a slow smile. "Please proceed. I don't see how a little *information* could do us any harm."

Apparently oblivious to the tension between the two, Jack turned his attention back to the boats.

"Why are you talking so funny?" Jonas whispered to Catherine as she held his arm in a death grip. "I suppose you think that low voice is sexy? Are you putting the moves on Big Jack?"

"Shh! Don't speak so loudly." She glared at him. "What

are you doing here? How did you find me?"

"I've been following you ever since you left my office."

"*What?* I knew it. You just want to ruin everything."

"On the contrary," Jonas protested, his lips turning up at the corners with mirth. "This is the best entertainment I've had in weeks. Please . . . let the show continue."

Cat eyed him suspiciously. Apparently his earlier anger was under control. The old Jonas, playful and dangerous, was back.

"All our boats are thur-o-ly inspected after each trip, so we're safe enough," Jack was telling them. "If there's any trouble, though, we've got a radio system an' backup that's sure t' get help on the way. There's Coast-Guard-approved life jackets, too, plus a bail-out dinghy, first aid equipment, fire extinguishers, bilge pumps, an' anything else you might need. We're right off the coast here, so as rescue doesn't take long if it's needed." He looked quite proud. It did not seem to occur to him for a moment that the manner in which he presented this information might do little to inspire the confidence of would-be charterers.

As Big Jack continued to extol the virtues of his fleet of boats, Catherine stewed. She let him ramble on and on, no longer feeling confident about what to say. With Jonas present, she felt less like a private detective and more like a truant child caught in the act of skipping class. That confounded man! And why did he have to show up just as she was about to get the information she needed? And why was he here in the first place?

"O' course, if you go out on the boat, yer gonna wanna have towels and so on," Jack was informing them. "That's extra. Each set o' towels is fifteen dollars. That's two fer the bath, two fer yer face, and two fer the hands. If you want bedding, that's two sheets, two blankets, an' two pillacases fer twenty-five dollars." He stopped only momentarily for breath. "Fishin' poles is extra. Is either one o' you a fisherman?" This last part he threw casually over his shoulder.

Jonas looked at Catherine with a glint in his eye. "Uh . . . *she* is," he said. His lips twitched as Catherine's eyes opened wide in horror. "In fact, she's a very good fisherman—or should I say *fisherwoman?* Aren't you, honey? Why don't you tell Jack about some of the big fish you've caught?"

"That's a lie!" Catherine hissed it under her breath so only Jonas could hear.

Jonas kept his voice just as low. "And what you're doing isn't?" He took her hand firmly in his. Under Jack's watchful eye, she dared not pull away. "I don't know what you're up to, Cat," he said quietly. "But I'm going to be right here to see what happens. Since you made it necessary for me to come all the way out here, I figure I might as well have a little fun. Besides, this is what happens when you lie. . . ."

Cat stared at him. She couldn't figure out what he was up to. Clearly, he was still upset with her for the accusations she had made. But was it her imagination, or was he enjoying this too?

By now, Jack had stopped giving them his sales pitch and now stood with hands on hips, regarding Catherine with a look of disbelief.

"You don't look like no fisherman to me," he said doubtfully.

Catherine couldn't blame him. In her silk blouse and high-heeled shoes, she appeared every inch the urban professional.

"Tell him about the time you caught a thirty-five pound Chinook on two-pound test," Jonas urged.

Cat just glared at him. Big Jack stared at her.

"Or . . . oh! Oh! Tell him about the time you got a sixty-pound flounder off the coast of Alaska," Jonas suggested, every bit the proud fiancé.

Catherine searched her mind desperately for some way out of this situation. "We really don't have time for that, *sugar lips*," she said pointedly to Jonas, then turned to Jack and said demurely, "I'm sure you have much better fishing stories than I do. Besides, all my best stories are about the ones that got away. What *I'd* really like is to hear some more about having a wedding on one of your boats." She artfully turned the conversation back in the direction she wanted it to go. "I'm not quite sure how that would work. Can you tell me if anyone else has planned something like this recently?"

Now that she had—ironically—earned his respect, Catherine found Big Jack to be much more helpful than he had been on the phone. "Well, now, a young couple did come in here a coupla weeks ago, lookin' t' do the same thing yer talkin' about here."

"Oh, really?" Catherine heard her voice rise up to its normal tone. Consciously, she made an effort to lower it. "You don't say?"

"That's right. They wanted t' get married just the two of 'em. Real romantic-like. Figured then they'd just sail away for a few days together after that." He gave Catherine a knowing glance. "Sounded like they wanted to get away from their families real bad, if you know what I mean. Poor kids."

Jonas made a choking noise. Catherine threw him a speaking glance that caused him to quickly get a grip on himself.

"So, were they looking at the *Mighty Mouse* too?" Cat asked Jack. If that was true, she knew she was safe. The boat had not left the harbor. Daphne and Elliott had to still be in the city.

"Can't really say," Jack said thoughtfully. "Thing is, I talk

126

to a lotta couples ever' week. Coulda been this boat they was lookin' at. Then again, it might not."

Catherine tried to control her impatience. "Well, do you think you wrote it down? Could you look at your records?" And then, at the suspicious look Jack gave her: "I'm, uh . . . really curious."

"Hmm. I kin give it a try." After giving her a look that made it clear he considered her to be a very odd woman indeed—an impression Catherine was becoming accustomed to making with strangers—he went back into the office to check his schedule. For the first time since her "fiancé's" arrival, she and Jonas found themselves alone.

It came not a moment too soon. Catherine was on the verge of exploding with anger. " 'Tell him about the time you went deep-sea fishing off the coast of Alaska,' " she hissed. "What on earth do you think you're doing?"

Jonas did not look the least bit ashamed of his behavior. "I might very well ask you the same thing."

"Don't be silly. You *know* what I'm doing. I'm trying to stop my sister from making the biggest mistake of her life."

"And that would be—?"

Catherine closed her eyes against the afternoon sun. Why wouldn't the man just cooperate? Or at least go away. Why did he have to make things so hard for her?

"That mistake would be marrying into a family that can only hurt her."

"I see."

Cat opened her eyes again as Jonas stepped even nearer. He was so close that she had to tip her neck back in order to look up at him. As she did, Jonas locked his eyes on hers, and she was unable to bring herself to look away. "I gather that's a mistake you weren't willing to make?"

She shook her head slightly, looking troubled. "What's

that supposed to mean?"

"Exactly what it sounds like, Cat." Jonas's voice was strong and filled with conviction. "You ended a relationship with me almost twelve years ago. I think I deserve to know why."

Her eyes flickered across the strong, well-defined features of his face—features she had once loved so dearly. Features that still made appearances in her dreams. "I didn't end it," she protested. "*You* ended it—when you decided to team up with your dad, even after all he'd done."

"He was my *father*." Jonas's eyes begged her to understand.

"He was a crook."

He threw his arms up in disbelief and frustration. "Is that *still* all you have to say? That's the best reason you have? Look, my dad made some mistakes, Cat. Okay, he made a *lot* of them. But did that mean I was supposed to disown him?"

"Did it mean you had to become just like him?"

Jonas's skin paled under his deep summer tan. "What are you saying?"

"Jonas, don't you see? I couldn't trust your father after what happened. And you . . . you're just like him! You have his charm, obviously his flair for success . . . you even *look* like him a little." Her eyes drank in the sight of his strong physique, curly brown hair, warm brown eyes.

"I had already lost my mother," she said matter-of-factly, taking several steps away. It was impossible to think clearly with Jonas standing so close to her. "My father nearly crumbled. I was responsible for three younger sisters. I couldn't afford to get my heart broken, to allow myself to fall for someone who ultimately would let us down too. . . ."

"What do you mean, let you down too?" Jonas followed her to the water's edge and laid one hand upon her arm in gesture of comfort. "Who let you down, Cat?"

"Your father."

Jonas nodded. "I know. Who else?"

Catherine's thoughts whirled. She did not know what to tell him. She could not think . . .

"Your mom, Catherine? Did your mother let you down, too, by dying? And your dad, too, by being so broken up he could barely take care of you girls?"

"Don't be silly." Catherine spun around to face Jonas. The look she gave him was cold. "Dying wasn't Mother's fault. She didn't want to die. Not then. And Dad . . . well, he did the best he could. . . ." Her voice trailed off. His hand still rested on her arm.

"You're right," Jonas agreed. "They both did their best. But they still weren't there for you, were they?"

Cat's eyes filled with tears she did not want to shed. "N-no," she admitted.

"And you needed them, didn't you?" Drawing a deep breath, Catherine tried to shake his arm away, but Jonas held her within a firm, painless grip. "Don't run away, Cat. Answer me."

Angrily, she did. "Of course I needed them. What little girl doesn't need her parents? But I managed, didn't I? I took care of myself."

"Guess you did." Jonas looked down at her with eyes filled with compassion. "The way you took care of yourself by walking away from me. I don't know . . . maybe it was the only thing you could do. But you should know, I loved you, Cat." She winced as he spoke the words. "I truly did. You may have thought you were protecting yourself. But I'm telling you now—all you did was walk away from someone who cared more for you than for anyone else in this world. I would not have lied to you, Cat. And I wouldn't have double-crossed you. You could have trusted me. And you may not like me anymore, but you *still* can trust me."

The thought came to Cat, wildly, that this was the answer she'd been looking for. "Then tell me what you know," she said, looking up at him earnestly. "Tell me where Daphne and Elliott went. Go with me to talk some sense into them. Maybe then I can believe you."

Jonas shook his head sorrowfully. "I can't do that, Cat."

"Why not?"

"You know why not. For exactly the reasons we've been talking about. My brother trusted me with information that I'm not at liberty to share—at least, not now. If I thought you just wanted to put your arms around Daphne and tell her you love her, I might change my mind. But the way you're approaching the situation right now . . ."

"What *about* the way I'm approaching the situation?" Catherine reacted sharply. The veiled accusation cut her to the core.

"Catherine." He squeezed the fingers of her right hand, but she remained cool and unresponsive. She could tell by the look in his eyes that this hurt him. But she could not bring herself to meet him even partway. It had been too long. The rift was too great. Old feelings could do nothing for them now. Why didn't he see that?

"Oh, Cat," he sighed. Her head spun at the intimate tenderness in his voice, and she felt herself being pulled back into her old feelings for him. "This isn't about Daphne. And it isn't about Elliott. Or my dad. Or me. This is about you. Your need to be in control of everything around you. You can't stand the fact that your sister is doing something without your permission, and you want to set her straight."

The words pulled her out of her romantic reverie. "And what's wrong with that?"

"Only you can answer that," he said. "But I think you know I won't respond to an ultimatum. Think about it, Cat. Once, you wanted me to walk away from my father. Now, you want me to betray my brother—which, if I did, would simply prove that I'm the sort of man you have worried that I would turn out to be."

Was this true? Catherine felt confused by this turning of her own logic upon her.

"I'm an honorable man, Cat," he told her soberly. "You can believe it. Not because I prove it according to *your* rules, but because of the way I live my life." He raised his hand now to her cheek and, for the briefest of moments, let it rest there, and gave her a quirky, sad smile. "I'm really not that bad when you get to know me . . . *if* you get to know me—"

Catherine had opened her mouth to speak, though she was unsure of what she was about to say, when Big Jack made a loud—and ill-timed—return.

"Looks like we didn't make a reservation for those young'ns at all," the man said, glancing down at the schedule he held in one fist.

Catherine's heart leaped at the news. "You mean they canceled? They didn't go through with it?" She grinned at Jonas, who eyed her uncertainly. "Did you hear that, *snooglepuss?* They didn't charter a boat after all!" Without thinking, she squeezed the hand of the man who was standing alarmingly close to her. Now, more than ever, they probably appeared to Big Jack to be a truly legitimate couple.

"Nope. Nope, they didn't charter no boat. I remember it real clear now. They was the couple that had the little problem."

"Little . . . problem?" Cat's smile grew stiff. She gave Jack a look of concern. "What sort of problem? Everything was all right, wasn't it?"

"Oh, sure. Nothin' a little Dramamine can't fix."

"They got . . . seasick?" Catherine could not believe her ears. Daphne had never had such a problem before.

"Not the bride." Jack gave them a toothy grin. "Just the groom."

Jonas clutched his stomach sympathetically and whispered in Catherine's ear: "Family curse."

Cat glanced from one man to the other in confusion. "So, the wedding was . . . canceled? Altogether?"

"Naw," Jack told her. Her face fell. "Just the part about the boat. They decided to go ahead and get married on land."

"Did they happen to say *where* on land?" she asked wearily, stepping away from Jonas once more.

"They didn't have any idea what to do next," Big Jack said again. "Poor kids."

"I see." Catherine turned away from him, understanding that she would have to accept defeat at last. She was just about to thank him for his time and tell him she'd get back to him if she found there was a need when he made the first statement that could actually be of some help to her.

"Lucky for that young couple, I have a friend that runs a little place over on Santa Catalina. They have weddin's in the garden a couple o' times a year. It seemed to be just what they wuz lookin' fer, so I told the kids I'd give my friend a call."

Catherine stared at him. "What kind of place? You mean, like a bed-and-breakfast?"

"That's right. It's a real nice one too. You folks'd like it."

"But I thought Ell—" Catherine stopped herself short. What would Big Jack say if she suddenly knew the name of the other woman's fiancé? "Er . . . *el groomo* was the kind to get seasick." Jonas began to cough and sputter. Cat slapped him on the back—*soundly*—as he tried to regain his composure. "Wouldn't they have to take one of the ferries over?"

"Most people do," Jack agreed. "You can get there by sea, leaving from Newport Harbor, Long Beach, San Pedro . . . even San Diego. But if money's no object . . ." He gave Cat and Jonas a rather hungry look that seemed to imply that he wondered if, in fact, money was no object for them—and was reconsidering the wisdom of sending his meal ticket elsewhere. ". . . there's the Island Express Helicopter Service. And there's seaplanes and air charters departing daily from Long Beach Airport or LAX—they's a little cheaper. You kin get there, all right," he said helpfully. "Where there's a will, I guar-un-tee there's a way."

Just as I thought, Catherine told herself, her spirits brightening considerably. "But, of course, for you . . ." Jack continued, "If you wanna go to Catalina, *I* kin take you."

"Thank you very much, Big Jack," Catherine said. "You've been a *world* of help. I'll give you a call if we decide to charter one of your boats. I must confess," she said lowering her voice, "that my wedding date is a bit up in the air."

"Oh. I see." After the way she and Jonas had been muttering under their breath to one another, the captain didn't look surprised. "Well, you just give Big Jack a call when that time comes."

"Thank you." Catherine smiled. "And in the meantime, if it isn't too much trouble—?"

Jack nodded knowingly. "La Puebla Inn. Ask for Chuck."

Cat grinned. "Thanks. You're a dear."

"You're welcome. And Miss?"

"Yes?"

He grinned. "Tell that sister o' yers Big Jack says good luck."

EIGHT

"I hate to fly. You know that? I mean, I really hate to fly."

The words were all but drowned out by the loud whirring of the helicopter, but Cat knew what Felicia was saying. Her sister had uttered the phrases so many times since fastening her seat belt, they'd become for her a kind of rosary. Now her face contorted with worry, Fee opened her pocketbook and began flipping through page after page filled with wallet-sized photographs of her children.

Cat leaned over and spoke loudly over the noise, "Fee, you *must* try to relax. You'll see the kids again, I promise." Catherine willed herself to be tolerant. She knew Felicia was going through a lot these days. Robert was harsh and demanding, and the children were more than a handful. As a teenager, Fee had been strong of character and filled with positive self-esteem. Since her wedding, however, her confidence in herself seemed to have been slowly but seriously drained away.

Fee looked up at her, glanced past her at the blue sky and ocean outside, blanched, then quickly looked down again at her photos. Despite her impatience, Cat's heart filled with compassion. Felicia didn't talk much about her personal struggles, even to her older sister. This troubled, yet at the same time relieved, Cat. When it got right down to it, she didn't know how to advise Felicia. Cat believed in the sanctity of marriage and couldn't urge her sister to leave the husband who treated her so poorly. At the same time, she could not help wishing Felicia's life could be different.

"I don't see why we had to come," Lucy shouted from the seat behind them.

"Fee, honey," Cat repeated, ignoring Lucy, "we're absolutely fine. The helicopter will be landing in less than ten minutes. Take a deep breath and just think about how great it's going to be in Catalina. Remember how much you used to enjoy it as a little girl."

Felicia breathed deeply as she was instructed, while Lucy leaned closer and said disapprovingly, "Don't make this sound like a vacation when it's not. You know the minute we touch down, you're going to be off and running to this B & B of yours."

"So?" Cat shouted back, "What's the problem? That's what we're here for."

"The problem is, it's not very honest of you to pretend this is a pleasure trip."

Catherine ignored the verbal jab and focused on patting Felicia's sleeve. Lucy had been prickly ever since Cat stopped by to pick her up that morning. Catherine guessed she felt guilty about revealing what little she knew about Daphne's elopement. Whereas Lucy had, at the end of their last conversation, sounded relieved to know that Cat was going in search of their youngest sister, today she seemed to have reverted to her original position: that they should leave Daphne alone and let her make her own decisions.

"I'm not a child, you know," Felicia said, clearly trying to put on a brave face. "I'm just a little scared, that's all. I'll be fine."

Catherine ceased her patting, sat back, and considered the sister who was closest to her in age. Felicia *was* scared, but she would be fine as soon as they touched ground. There was no need to hold her hand . . . literally or figuratively. She smiled sympathetically at Fee, then sat back against her own seat and focused on the churning waters in the ocean beneath her.

Within minutes, the noise and motion of the chopper had lulled her into a state of semiwakefulness. The little bit of rest was much needed; she hadn't slept much the night before. Her thoughts had been consumed by her worries about Daphne . . . and her frustration toward the curiously intriguing, though still completely irritating, Jonas Riley.

There was no denying it: Something had stirred within her. She disliked him, distrusted him. He represented everything she hated: fear, uncertainty, grief, and loss. If only she could forget he existed and get on with her life!

Except . . . the question haunted her: Had she ever, really, gotten on with her life after losing Jonas? After walking away from the relationship, had she ever been the same? Over the past week, she had become increasingly aware of the fact that she'd spent the last decade in emotional limbo. Davis's and Lucy's questions had reminded her that she'd had no romantic relationships worth speaking of. Her friendships were limited to relationships with her family and casual interactions with acquaintances at work, at the gym, at the various civic organizations she was part of, and the church she attended on Sundays. Had it all been worth the sacrifice? Had the safe world she had built for herself been worth the emptiness she now faced?

"You may have thought you were protecting yourself. But I'm telling you now—all you did was walk away from someone who cared more for you than for anyone else in this world. You could have trusted me, Cat. I loved you."

Suddenly, Cat found herself standing, once more, before Jonas at the pier. "Do you love me, Cat?" He reached out with one hand and stroked the gentle slope of her cheek. "It's been twelve years.

Can you tell me now? Did it really end? Or do you love me still?"

As if of their own volition, Catherine's arms reached up and secured themselves around his strong, masculine neck. She closed her eyes and turned her face upward as Jonas lowered his, and in the moment she'd been waiting for nearly half her life, their reunion was sealed with a pure and holy kiss . . .

"Cat? Cat?"

Catherine kept her eyes shut tight. How very odd. If Jonas was kissing her, how could he be calling her name? And why was his voice so . . . high-pitched? It really wasn't attractive at all. Something didn't seem right. A moment later, she was sure of this fact when her mind registered the faint distinct sound of giggling close to her ear.

"Sorry, Sleeping Beauty," Lucy told her in a voice that was anything but apologetic. "Just thought you'd want to know we're about to land."

"Oh." Cat blinked away the last vestiges of her dream and began to gather up her things. "Great."

"You don't really sound like you think it's so great," Lucy said. She was hanging over Catherine's seat back and speaking loudly over the noise. "Did I interrupt a nice dream?"

Catherine shrugged noncommittally. "Not particularly," she fibbed, hoping to avoid her sister's interrogation.

"That's too bad." Lucy studied her closely. "I just thought maybe I had, because you were saying something that looked an awful lot like 'I love you—' "

"No!" Cat gaped at her. "I did *not* say that!"

"No? Okay. Must've been my mistake," Lucy told her loudly. "But I'm telling you, as a professional matchmaker, it's my job to know love. And you were looking pretty dopey, my dear. I know that face: It's the face of a woman who's fallen . . . *hard.*"

Appearing thoroughly satisfied, she leaned back in her own seat, leaving Cat to process her words. Next to Catherine, Felicia remained oblivious to the conversation that had taken place as she focused her attention on checking the security of her seat belt, putting her children's pictures away, and watching the landing-related activities that were going on all around her.

Cat felt a wave of panic wash over her. Had she really talked in her sleep? Or had Lucy simply made a lucky guess? Lucy had always maintained that Catherine and Jonas should never have broken up. Ever since dinner the week before, she had been making sly little comments about the two of them. She was probably just teasing . . . trying to get Catherine to admit she still cared for the man. Which she didn't . . . did she?

Then again, maybe there was some truth to what Lucy said. Catherine had, after all, been dreaming about Jonas. Not just about him, but about *reuniting* with him. If she could dream that she and Jonas were getting back together, couldn't she have dreamt that she loved him?

It was possible, she conceded. But even if she *had* dreamed about the emotion, did dreaming about it make it true? Like everyone else, Catherine had crazy dreams on a regular basis. As a teenager, she'd dreamed that she'd married Shaun Cassidy. A few months ago, she had dreamed that she was skydiving naked. None of those dreams held any shred of truth. Why should she assume that her dream about Jonas had any special meaning?

Pleased with this sensible conclusion to her inner debate, Catherine turned her attention out the window to the mass of land that was growing larger with every second of their approach.

Ah, Catalina . . . my island. Her heart began to race, as it had whenever she had arrived on the island as a child. At the time, of course, she, her mother, and her sisters had made the journey via ship, and not helicopter. Cat could almost feel the misty air—damp from the sea—on her face as she remembered. And her mother's face, which had started to grow dim and misty in her memory, was suddenly fresh and clear again.

Mother. The memory made Cat feel both happy and unsettled, somehow vulnerable.

For Cat's mother had loved this island. She and the girls—and Edward, when his work schedule allowed it—had spent a great deal of their free time here together, as a family. Now Catherine's mind filled with images of herself as a child: exploring tiny coves with her siblings, skipping along the beachfront's serpentine wall, and splashing in the clear water that lapped at the girls' legs as they played in the safety of Avalon Harbor.

All that had stopped when her mother died. Cat's father had been far too busy and distracted to take the girls, and she herself had been too young to plan and organize such a complicated outing. Not that she would have done it even if she could have. It would have seemed wrong to go without her mother. But Cat's memories of her times there remained sacred; they represented, for her, the simplest, most joyous moments of her childhood—in fact, of her entire life.

In her mind's eye she could see her mother gathering them all together on the boat to explain exactly where they were going and how this place related to the world where they lived. Before Cat was five years old—before Lucy or Daphne had even been born—she had known that Santa Catalina was one of the eight Santa Barbara Channel Islands off the coast of Southern California. Her mother explained that, though the journey took some time, they really were not traveling all that far; Catalina was only twenty-six miles off the mainland coast.

This had meant little to Cat. "Twenty-six" was just a number . . . and she had seen the magical place with her own eyes. Like Treasure Island, or the land of Ali Baba and the forty thieves, Santa Catalina was a world completely unlike the one in which she lived her everyday life.

And it was true, in a way. Though Catalina was not a tropical island—and in fact, had a climate not unlike that of nearby Southern California—its topography was vastly different. Like the land surrounding Hollywood, Santa Catalina had its share of gentle, rolling hills. However it also was characterized by steeply rising mountains, unlike any found on the Southern California mainland, as well as beaches, meadows, and valleys. After some of the family's excursions to the rugged, windward side of the island, Cat used to imagine that a giant had come along and scooped up large cliffs, dropping them right alongside the ocean's edge. It reminded her of a place where the Road Runner might step aside and trick Wile E. Coyote into falling into the sea.

Cat particularly liked it when her mother told her how she had been named after the island. Though Edward had balked at actually naming the child "Catalina" after Santa Catalina —Spanish for "St. Catherine"—he had agreed to Catherine, the next best thing. As a child, Catherine had felt a strong sense that the island she was named for was indeed, in some way, her very own.

And she had loved learning the story of her island from her mother. Anna Salinger had been a brilliant woman, well-read in subjects such as literature and history, and this knowledge served her well when her firstborn deluged her with requests for stories about "Cat's island." She had told her oldest child —and, later, her three younger children—about the Gabrielino Indians, who lived in primitive homes at the modern sites of Little Harbor, Avalon, and Two Harbors. From their mother, the girls had learned that the friendly, hardworking Indians went about naked or wore aprons made out of otter skins, and that they kept strange animals for pets: dogs that howled but did not bark.

With her children gathered eagerly about her knees, the girls' mother recounted tales of early Spanish explorers who claimed the island for motherland Spain and who sailed its waters hunting the sea otter, coveted for its soft, velvety fur. Pirates, too, had frequented the island, she told her openmouthed audience, explaining how the seafaring robbers would hide their plunder on its shores while evading capture. These stories led directly to many years' worth of gleeful treasure hunts involving hidden coves, vast stretches of sand, and handmade maps in which a bold X marked the spot.

Catherine let her eyes linger upon the beauty of the island's main city, which she could barely see in the distance, located on the Bay of Avalon. The great white walls and rust-colored roof of the enormous, perfectly round Casino now glistened in the sun. Along the bay, the city of Avalon sat nestled against the steep hills of Catalina's eastward coastline. A feeling of nostalgic longing swept over her as she pictured herself walking—or rather, climbing—the once familiar, winding streets that were so like those found in the sun-drenched Mediterranean villages she once visited during a vacation with college friends.

Moments later, they had landed at a helipad approximately three quarters of a mile outside of the city. As they'd been told to do, they flagged a taxi and were soon on their way to Avalon.

"We're heading for La Puebla Inn," Catherine told the driver. "I believe it's on Catalina Avenue, just off Crescent?"

The man—a tan, bulky individual in his early forties, with

sun-bleached hair—nodded wordlessly, and Catherine settled back against the passenger seat beside him. In the back,
Lucy and Felicia were talking animatedly about the confrontation that was about to occur.

"I'm just saying," Lucy was telling her sister, "that we
shouldn't be too hard on Daphne. This isn't the end of the
world, you know. It's not like she's hurting anybody. She's
just getting married, not joining a cult."

"There's no such thing as *just* getting married," Felicia
argued, her ability to converse normally much improved
since getting out of the helicopter. "And how do you know
she's not hurting anybody? She could very well be hurting
herself. Who knows?"

Catherine remained facing front, letting the comment go
unchallenged. She recognized the thinly veiled reference to
Felicia's own marriage, but this was neither the time nor the
place to discuss it. Judging from the silence that followed
Fee's warning, Lucy apparently shared her point of view.
"And then of course," Felicia continued in a stage whisper,
"there's *you know who . . .*"

Cat pretended that she hadn't heard. *'You know who,'
indeed.* How ironic. It was funny, really, how the scenario was
being played out. She, Catherine, was worried about her sisters, who were in turn worried about her . . . for worrying
about one of them. What a vicious circle.

As they entered the city limits, she turned her mind to
reviewing the few facts she had. She knew that Big Jack had
referred Daphne and Elliott to his friend's bed-and-breakfast, the La Puebla Inn. Cat also knew that the newlywed-
wannabes had not yet checked into the B & B—at least under
their real names. This she had discovered the night before
when trying to reach them via telephone. The clerk had
insisted that no so such party had registered.

"Are you sure?" Catherine had pressed him. "They may be traveling under a different name. It's a young couple. She has dark, curly hair. He . . ." She hesitated. It had been years since she'd seen Elliott Riley, and at the time he'd been only thirteen. "He's . . . got dark hair." She paused. "I think."

"Ma'am, I am sorry." The young man did sound genuinely apologetic. "But we have six different couples staying here. And, as luck would have it, you have described practically all of them. I think."

"Well, could you just ask them—?"

"No, ma'am. Again, I am very sorry. I am not authorized to give you any more information than that."

Catherine let out a heavy sigh. "All right, then. May I speak with your owner? Chuck? I was referred by a friend of his: Jack . . . um, Jack . . ." Cat flushed with embarrassment. She didn't even have a last name. "Big Jack," she finished lamely.

"Oh yes, Big Jack!" This brought forth an enthusiastic response. "Yes, Jack is one of our favorite guests. But I'm sorry. Chuck isn't here tonight. He's at the mainland and won't be home until tomorrow morning. If you'd like to check back then . . . ?"

And so Cat had dragged Fee, willingly, and Lucy, kicking and screaming, on an early-morning jaunt to Avalon. She wasn't even sure why she felt the need to have them with her . . . for moral support, she supposed. Or to help her feel more justified in taking off work in the middle of the week. But Felicia had located a baby-sitter and seemed glad of a rare outing without the children, especially to a spot she remembered as vividly as Cat did. Lucy had come mostly because she had promised to come, although Cat suspected that the prospect of visiting the scene of childhood jaunts swayed her a bit as well.

The taxi came to a stop at an old Spanish-style villa flanked by palm and elderberry trees. Out front, a carefully tended rock garden provided a home for a wide assortment of wildflowers native to Catalina: Indian paintbrush, woodland star, wild four o'clock, and heliotrope. The outside walls of the large house were painted a soft Southwestern pastel pink. Orange Spanish-tile shingles covered the roof, and cheerful white balconies fronted two of the upstairs rooms.

Catherine slipped the driver a handful of bills, turned to her sisters, and said with as much confidence as she could muster: "All right, girls. Let's go!"

With a hearty slam of the taxi door, she stepped up onto the sidewalk and led the way to the front door of the inn. More timidly—or reluctantly—her sisters followed.

As she stepped inside, Catherine found herself in a short hallway leading to a modified lobby area.

"This place is beautiful!" Felicia breathed.

"Look at the furniture! It's all from the twenties," said Lucy, who knew about such things. "I'll bet that's when the house was built."

At first, no one appeared. But as the sound of their voices filled the hall, a young man appeared from a doorway that led off to the left.

"Hello. May I help you?" he offered and stepped behind the desk in order to do so.

Catherine considered the youth in front of her, sizing up whether he would be of any real use to her. She wondered if he was the same clerk who had helped her on the telephone the night before.

"Yes, I believe so," she said in her most businesslike voice. It was time to pull rank. No more Ms. Nice Guy. "My name is Catherine Salinger. I'm here to see Chuck—" She blinked.

No last name again. "Um . . . Chuck. It's a matter of utmost importance."

"Oh." The young man did not appear to know what to do with this bit of information. "I'm sorry. Chuck's not here."

Cat stared. The whole sordid adventure was beginning to feel like a comedy of errors. This was an outcome that had not even occurred to her.

Last night, the clerk had sworn that Chuck would be back from the mainland the next day. What was the problem? It was *now* the next day. Only . . .

Cat suddenly felt sick. In her eagerness, she had booked reservations on the first helicopter to depart San Pedro that morning. There was no way Chuck could have beaten them over if he'd gone by water. Even if he had taken the first Catalina Express boat to leave Long Beach, at 6:45 A.M., he would be arriving at the inn at nearly the same time she and her sisters did. If he took a later boat, the ninety-minute trip would not bring him into Avalon until sometime after ten.

"Well, then . . ." She reached for Felicia's purse.

Fee tightened her grip, giving Cat a wounded glare. "What do you think you're doing?"

"Getting your wallet."

"What? I don't think you have to bribe the man—"

"*Fee.*" Catherine pulled insistently upon the handle of her sister's purse. "I'm not taking your money, for goodness' sake. I just want to get a picture. You have hundreds of your kids. Don't you have any of Daphne?"

"Not any recent ones," Fee said, now sounding apologetic.

Catherine flipped through page after page of plastic encased photos. Finally she found one, circa 1989, that bore a slight resemblance to their "missing person." "Here," she said, thrusting the picture under the man's nose. "Have you seen this girl before? Picture better teeth, more fashion sense. Hair sort of like my sister's here." She waved in Lucy's direction.

The man glanced obediently at both picture and sister but shook his head. "I don't think so. I'm afraid I can't help you. And neither can Chuck. You see—"

"I know, I know. Your boss isn't here. All right, then," Catherine said, making a snap decision. "We'll just have to wait for him. Do you have a sitting room?"

"Well, yes," the clerk said nervously. "But first I have to tell you—"

"Is it that way?" she asked, pointing to the hallway from which he had come.

"Yes, it is," he told her. "But, as I said, you won't need to wait there. You see—"

"That's all right. We'll find our way," said Catherine. "Come on, girls."

Out of the corner of her eye, she saw Lucy throw the young man an apologetic glance. She threw back an irritated glare as the man explained something in urgent tones while Lucy listened with what was, apparently, great interest.

Without missing a step, Catherine made her way down the hall in the direction of the sitting room. *Oh, Lucy. That's not the way to get things done. By the time Chuck finally gets here, you're going to know that boy's whole life story.* She stepped into the open doorway and scanned the bright, open sitting area, which was decorated with exquisite antiques, lovingly restored to their original beauty. *Meanwhile, I will have done enough detective work to make sure I find—*Catherine came to an abrupt halt in the doorway, and her mouth fell open wide.

"JONAS?"

Jonas Riley rose from the couch where he'd been seated and stretched out his arms wide. "In the flesh!" he said cheerfully. He gave no indication that he was aware of Catherine's distress. He looked nothing like a man determined to drive her crazy. An onlooker who was unaware of their personal history would take him to be nothing more than a relaxed vacationer, ready to take in the sights of Catalina. He certainly looked the part: khaki shorts, moccasins, and a short-sleeved, button-up shirt, untucked, that was patterned with orange and red lobsters.

Realizing that she looked like a fish on dry land, Catherine snapped her mouth shut and blinked her wide-open eyes while searching for words. It would not do for him to see how thoroughly he unnerved her.

"You look like you should be back at college," she said, surveying his youthful attire. Immediately she longed to retrieve the words, though she was not sure why. Would he take them as a criticism or a compliment?

"*You* look like you should be in the pages of a fashion magazine," Jonas said appreciatively. There was no mistaking the approval in his tone.

Cat blushed. In her rush to get ready that morning, she'd thrown on the first thing she pulled out of her closet, a pair of flax-colored linen jeans and matching white shirt. On her feet were simple brown calfskin clogs. There had been no time for makeup other than a bit of pale pink lipstick and a single coat of mascara. Her honey-colored hair, which she usually wore pinned back, was loose today, a detail that clearly had not escaped Jonas's notice. Catherine watched as his eyes traveled from her clothes to her face to the wavy golden mane that hung about her shoulders and back to meet her eyes. He blushed, seeing that he had been caught drinking in her features. But instead of feeling superior at the revelation of his vulnerability, Cat simply felt quietly and deeply pleased.

"I—I don't understand," she finally managed. "How did you get here so fast?"

"Seaplane. And you?"

"Helicopter."

Silence fell between them as each considered a next move. The standoff continued as the other members of Cat's party joined them.

"Well, look who's here!" Lucy exclaimed. Wisely, she refrained from laughing out loud, but amusement could clearly be seen in her bright blue eyes. Her short, chestnut curls bounced as she turned her head quizzically to one side. "Why, you were right, Darrell," she said, addressing the clerk. "There *was* someone back here, waiting to see us. Thank you for saying so." She looked at Catherine smugly.

"I am sorry," the man told Cat, offering up what was quickly becoming his trademark phrase. "I tried to tell you, but—"

"That's all right," Catherine said, sounding a bit more understanding than she had upon arrival. "I'm the one who should be embarrassed. I wasn't listening."

"I was going to tell you, but first I wanted to explain that there isn't any point in waiting here for Chuck. He called this morning, before you got here, to tell me that he won't be home until tomorrow."

Chuck won't be here until tomorrow. You've wasted a trip . . . again. Catherine shook her head dumbly. "But . . . why? Did he say where he's staying now? What he's doing on the mainland for another day? Where he could be reached?"

"He did not. I am—"

"I know. You're sorry." She gave him a weak smile, giving up at last. "Me too."

"Well, *I'm* not sorry," Jonas broke in.

"Of course you're not," Cat said somewhat bitterly. "This

is exactly what you wanted."

"As a matter of fact, that's true," he assured her. He moved across the room and stood at Cat's side. "But not the way you think."

"Please, Jonas," she said in a heavy voice. "I'm too tired, too frustrated, and too angry for games."

The smile faded from his face and he trained serious eyes upon her. "I'm not playing any game, Cat," he said pointedly. "You should know that by now."

"All right then, Jonas." She was finding it harder and harder to fight him. "I'll bite. Tell me why are you happy Chuck won't be back until tomorrow?"

"Because," he said, reaching out and taking Catherine's hand. The smile was back. "Now there is nothing to stop me from spending the day here with the three most beautiful ladies on Catalina Island."

Cat could not believe her ears. *Nothing, that is, except the fact that I don't want to spend the day with you.* But even as the protest formed in her mind, she knew it sounded phony. Though her mind believed the words, on some level her heart did not.

Felicia responded to the compliment like a flower feeling sunshine for the first time in weeks. She turned her face upward toward Jonas and beamed. "Why, thank you! What a sweet thing to say!"

Catherine felt a flash of jealousy rise within her and pushed it down just as quickly. *What's wrong with you, Cat,* she scolded herself. *The man means nothing to you, and goodness knows, Fee could use a little bit of an ego boost. I wonder when was the last time Robert said something nice to her.*

Lucy was not feeling so charitable. "Heel, Felicia," she said in a stage whisper.

Fee blushed but didn't say another word.

Jonas took it all in stride. "Nothing sweet about it," he said, laughing. "It's the truth. I've waited over twelve years for an opportunity to show the Salinger girls the town. It would be extremely unkind of you to deny me a pleasure so easily granted."

"It's too bad *Daphne* isn't here to join us," Cat said pointedly.

"Mmm. As you say." Jonas refused to rise to the bait. "I guess there's just that much more pressure on you, my dear Cat, to entertain me." He pulled her hand toward him and tucked it into the crook of his arm. Catherine blushed as she felt the warmth of his skin under her fingers. "And believe me, you *do* entertain me. Immensely."

"Me? Entertain you? Don't make me laugh." But Cat didn't feel like laughing. She felt . . . alarmingly excited. Thrilled, in fact, at the prospect that Jonas might find her amusing—might even crave her company. *And I thought Fee was an easy target? I've been out of the dating circuit too long if a few words from a weasel like Jonas can turn my head.*

Perhaps sensing that she was beginning to waver, Jonas pushed for an answer. "So what'll it be, Cat?" he asked persuasively. "Will you join me?"

"I can't, Jonas," she said. "You know that." But her voice reflected an uncertainty her words did not. Despite the anger she felt toward him, despite her worry for Daphne, she found that she did, indeed, want to spend the day with Jonas. In fact, she wanted that more than she had wanted anything in a very long time. For old times' sake, no doubt. But since when had she been so nostalgic?

"I've got to find my sister." She no longer sounded convinced.

"Of course," he said soberly. "And how will you do that?"

Catherine blinked at him, feeling acutely aware that her

hand still rested upon his arm. Should she remove it? Should she keep it in place? "I don't know."

"Hmm." Jonas thought about this. "Do you have any other leads?"

"No," Catherine admitted.

"Any other ideas?"

"Well . . . no."

"Do you know of a single person who is aware of where Daphne and Elliott have gone? Who might take you to them?" Suddenly it was very clear where this line of questioning was leading.

"Just . . . you," Cat said dryly.

"Hmm." Jonas withdrew her hand from his arm and began to wander around the room. He managed to keep his face straight, but Catherine could see he was enjoying himself. "It seems to me then—not that I'm an expert on such things, mind you—that you might be best served by spending the day with the one person who might actually be able to help."

"And that would be you."

"That," Jonas agreed, "as you say, would be me."

Catherine settled her hands on the gentle slope of her hips and regarded him shrewdly. "I think this is what's called blackmail."

"Don't be ridiculous, Cat. I'm not asking you for money."

"No. You're asking for my time," she accused him. "My attention. My *pardon*."

Jonas stopped pacing and looked at her, his eyes intense. "I may be asking for a lot more than that," he admitted, his voice soft and low.

Catherine shook her head. She had no idea what he was implying and had no intention of asking.

"Oh, I didn't mean anything bad by that," he amended quickly. "I simply want to show you ladies the town. Come on, Cat. Spend the day with me. Give me a chance."

She eyed him warily. "And if I do, you'll tell me where Daphne is?"

"I'm not saying that. No ultimatums . . . remember?"

"But you said I would be best served by—"

"I was teasing, Cat." He said gently. "Yes, I know where they are. But at this point, I'm still not sure whether or not I should tell you. Maybe later I'll feel more and more convinced that you are the loving woman I once knew and not an imperious control freak who—"

"Hey!" Catherine sputtered a protest.

"Sorry. I just mean that I'm beginning to trust your motives. I don't want those two kids to get hurt any more than you do."

Cat felt her resolve beginning to weaken. "Really?"

"Really."

Catherine weighed her two choices: go back to the mainland and sulk or spend a glorious day in Avalon. And sighed. Jonas was right. There wasn't anything else to do at home to find Daphne . . . and, feeling the way she did, she'd be too distracted to get any worthwhile work done. She wouldn't be able to talk to Chuck until the next day. All she could do now was wait . . . and worry. And wouldn't the waiting be a lot more bearable if she spent the time on her favorite island?

Her rationalization was growing with great speed now. *I've already taken off work. I never use my vacation days. And it seems almost sinful to waste the money I spent on the flight over. Besides, my sisters will be there with us. What's the worst that could happen?*

"Oh, all right," she said in a grudging voice. "If it's okay with Lucy and Fee, we'll stay."

"Actually, I think we're going to take off on our own," Lucy said quickly.

Fee gave her a strange look. "We are? I thought you—"

This earned her a sharp elbow poke to the ribs from Lucy. "Yes, we *are*. Remember? We just decided."

"We did? But I—"

"You see, Felicia and I rarely get any one-on-one girl time," Lucy explained to Jonas with exaggerated brightness. "You'll be doing us a favor really by getting Cat out of our hair."

Jonas grinned.

"Hey!" Cat sputtered again. "You didn't even want to—"

Lucy ignored her. "Then it's all decided. Don't worry about us, Cat. We'll get ourselves home. You two have a good time, and we'll talk to you tomorrow." With that, she grabbed Felicia's arm, and before her sister had the chance to offer up her own good-byes, the two were gone.

Jonas stared after them like a man who had just witnessed an alien landing. He scratched his head. "I hear Lucy owns a matchmaking business these days."

"Mmm-hm." Cat folded her arms across her chest and stared along with him.

Jonas considered this. "She's very good," he said at last.

"Mmm-hm," Catherine said, giving him an sheepish look. "Heaven help us, she is."

"Well, then." He grabbed her hand and, with a cheerful wave toward Darrell, the young clerk, started for the door. "I sure hope you can learn to like me, Cat. Because it's beginning to look like we haven't got a chance."

NINE

"All right. You have me now. What are you going to do with me?"

Out in the brilliant summer sunshine, away from the influence of the younger sisters who made her feel so old and responsible, Catherine felt an overwhelming desire to flirt outrageously. And after all, why shouldn't she? She was young, attractive—or so she was told on a regular basis by Davis Pierce—and unattached. She hadn't felt any particular loyalty to any one man since Jonas. But that was another issue altogether.

Buoyed by the look of delight and surprise her question elicited from her companion, Cat made an instant decision to loosen up for the rest of the day. There was nothing she could do about the situation involving Daphne. Besides, it had been far too long since she'd been to Catalina—and far too long since she'd enjoyed the company of an attractive man, even if it was Jonas Riley. She had the sun on her shoulders and all day to convince Jonas he could trust her with Elliott and Daphne's whereabouts. What possible harm could there be in letting herself relax for a few hours?

Only in the back of her mind was the familiar voice of suspicion still buzzing . . . *but what if they . . . what if he . . .* For the first time in many years she made the decision to ignore it, just for a while.

Instinctively she had pointed her feet toward the beach as they walked away from La Puebla Inn. Already they were at

Crescent Avenue, which paralleled the Bay of Avalon. Almost directly ahead was Pleasure Pier, which extended into the bay. There, she knew, they could stop for some chili at a popular hangout called Eric's, check the tide table at the harbormaster's office, obtain boat rental information, or hook up with a sightseeing tour. At Catherine's left, to the north, was the far end of the harbor where the Casino was located.

"I don't know," Jonas admitted. "What do you want to do?"

"I don't know," Cat echoed, sounding like a bored teenager. "What do *you* wanna do?"

Jonas laughed, a rich, hearty sound that filled Cat's ears and warmed her heart. "I'm not sure what our options are."

"What do you mean? Surely you've been to Catalina before?" Catherine looked horrified.

"Nope. Just never got around to it. I take it from the look of disgust you're giving me that you have?"

"Not in a long time," she confessed. "But I used to know this place like the back of my own hand."

"And speaking of your hands," Jonas said, playfully seizing one of them with his own, "I remember a time when *I* used to know them pretty well myself—"

"Whoa . . . whoa. Easy now, Casanova," she warned. It took great effort to keep herself from smiling. "This is a truce. A day of friendship, if you will. This is not, I repeat *not,* a date. Romance is definitely not on my mind."

"Liar," he teased.

"Lech," she smiled back. They gazed at each other shyly.

"I could have sworn you were flirting with me a minute ago."

"Wishful thinking," she said stubbornly.

"How intriguing. And what *were* you thinking?"

She laughed and gave him a playful punch to the arm. "Not me! *You.* *You* were thinking wishfully."

"Ahhh. I see. Forgive me. My mistake." He cast a glance around the bay. "So what *do* you want to do? Seriously."

Catherine looked ahead to Middle Beach, just to the north of the pier, where a group of delighted, screaming children were playing in the sand. In the water, about fifty feet out, was anchored a diving float with a slide, now in use by several older children and adult swimmers. Cat thought about this for a moment, then dismissed it, having not brought a bathing suit and feeling too cheap to buy another one.

"Well, we could go golfing, play some tennis. Go water-skiing, ride horses. Maybe do a little fishing—"

"Ooh, fishing. I hear *you're* quite a fisherwoman," Jonas said with a wink. "What shall it be? Sea bass? Rock cod? Button perch . . . ?"

Catherine ignored him. "Or we could just walk around, see the sights. Actually, I'd like to do that, sort of get reacclimated. How about if we walk a bit, up to North Beach? The water gets deep a lot quicker there, so parents generally keep the smaller children away. The tide's fairly low, too, so if we go even further up to those large rocks—see, there, along the boardwalk, just before the Casino?—we may be able to hunt crabs. We should have some hamburger though. They adore uncooked hamburger."

"Little savages."

Cat glanced behind them at the businesses on Crescent Avenue. "Why don't we walk over to one of those restaurants and buy some raw meat? My sisters and I used to do that as kids—"

"Ugh. Didn't your parents ever feed you?"

"—and feed it to the *crabs.*" Cat could not keep from

laughing out loud. She had forgotten how much she had once enjoyed spending time with Jonas. At the time, she'd thought he brought out the best in her. In his presence, she remembered being more lighthearted and playful than she'd ever been with anyone else.

But this, of course, was partly what made him so dangerous. For if Cat was not in control—and it was beginning to seem that when she was with Jonas, she still was not—who would be? Certainly not Jonas himself—as far as she could tell, he was still as impulsive and free-spirited as ever, feeling no qualms about abetting an ill-advised elopement or taking two days off work to follow her around. Someone had to be logical. Someone had to be reasonable. If not, both of them were bound to get hurt—just as they had been hurt twelve years before.

Catherine felt a sneaking suspicion that she was playing with fire. If she continued to spend time with Jonas, she would certainly become emotionally attached to him once again.

But . . . who was she kidding? Cat *already* was feeling drawn to him again. In spite of everything she knew, her heart still cared. She had spent more than a decade missing him, and she would miss him again when all this was over, when Daphne was back and safe and life was back in its familiar routine. But for now he was hers—if not to keep, then to enjoy for the day.

"Buy me some raw meat?" she asked hopefully.

"Milady's wish is my command." Jonas extended one leg out in front of him, threw an arm heavenward, then lowered both arm and body in a sweeping bow. Then Catherine watched as he made his way over to a line of customers waiting at the walk-up window of a nearby hamburger stand. Seeing him in this light, she found it hard to believe he was the same man who had been the target of her animosity for so many years.

"I don't think all the Rileys are bad." Isn't that what Daphne had said?

"Phooey," Cat grumbled. The sun must be making her lightheaded. In an attempt to regain control, she pulled her beloved cell phone out of her purse and dialed the office.

"Hi, Beauty," Davis Pierce said cheerfully when she finally got through. "Did you find our little rebel?"

"Not yet," Cat admitted. "And I think I'm going to be detained for a while."

"Good for you," Davis said approvingly. "By something fun, I hope."

"No," Cat lied, but her eyes and mind were on Jonas. Twenty feet away, he had struck up a conversation with a young skateboarder who stood in line behind him on the sidewalk. The two spoke easily together, as if they were peers. Catherine continued to watch Jonas as he interacted with the group of strangers around him, then the cashier behind the counter. She laughed at the expression the teenage girl gave him when he made his request. Jonas absently combed through his close-cropped curls with one hand as he talked. He made a joke. The young girl laughed. Catherine's heart surged with feelings she could not identify. For the moment, at least, all was well with her world.

"Cat, are you there?"

"Hmm. Oh, sorry, Davis. I think I'm going out of range." *Or out of my mind.* "I'll call you later."

"You do that, sweetie."

Cat snapped the flip phone shut and had it put away by the time Jonas returned.

"Raw meat, you say?" he said dubiously. "I'll have you know that girl behind the counter thought I was a regular loon."

"Mmm. How perceptive of her."

Jonas narrowed his eyes at her. "You're not just making up this thing about the crabs, are you? You know, to make me look foolish? This isn't like the old story about the moon being made of green cheese?"

She raised a hand in a solemn three-fingered salute. "Scout's honor, I swear, we really did feed bits of raw hamburger to the little shore crabs. Come on. I'll show you."

With one hand, Jonas clutched the brown bag filled with their "bait." They easily fell into step with one another. Though Jonas's legs were lanky, Catherine had always had an especially long stride and was able to keep up with very little effort.

Together they walked in silence along the boardwalk, in the direction of Casino Point. Soon Middle Beach, with its hoards of yelling children, was behind them. They walked by the arcade and the retaining wall bordering sandy North Beach, taking a short side trip down its steps to the water's edge. Like children, they slipped off their shoes and dipped their toes in the gentle surf.

"Ack!" Catherine squealed at the shock of the cold water. But in a moment her body adjusted to the temperature, and she was able to draw in her other foot.

Jonas waded in beside her and scanned the horizon. "What's that round thing down there?" he asked, pointing north. "What did you call it . . . the Casino? It's huge. You can't tell me that place is filled with people gambling?"

"No way. That thing? Look at the size of it." Catherine bent to roll up her pant legs so she could wander out further into the bay. "The entire population of the island could fit in there. Besides, it's not there for gambling."

"Then what's it for? And where'd it come from? I've never seen anything like it."

Proudly Catherine drew upon the information she had gleaned from her mother when she was just a child. "Originally, the island was owned by the Spaniards, then Mexico. Eventually, it ended up in the hands of the Santa Catalina Island Company. For a while, William Wrigley Jr.—you know, the chewing gum and baseball field guy?—was a major stockholder. He invested tons of money in the island. Probably the greatest part of it went into the Casino.

"There's a theater inside that goes back to the twenties—that's when the 'talkies' first came out and when the Casino was built. There's a huge ballroom, too, plus an art gallery and museum."

"I guess it's the most important building on the island."

"Pretty much."

Shielding his eyes against the sunlight bouncing off the Casino's outside walls, he mused, "So there's a ballroom, huh?"

"That's right."

"I'd like to take you dancing there someday."

Catherine hesitated.

"What's wrong? Don't you believe I can dance?"

"Of course I do. It's just that—"

"Because I can, you know. Just watch me." With an athlete's grace, Jonas slipped one hand against the small of her back; grasped her free hand in a loose but firm grip; and began to spin her about in the shallow water.

"Jonas!" Catherine caught her breath. "We're going to fall!" A second later, her prediction almost came true when he caught his bare toe on a sharp stone and stumbled.

"Sorry," he said, looking properly embarrassed, and began to shake off the water that had splashed up on his legs.

Laughing, Cat came out of the shallows and collected her shoes before heading back toward the boardwalk and resuming their beachfront journey.

The next landmark they passed was the Tuna Club, originally established near the turn of the century as a place for fishermen to swap stories about "the one that got away." Cat guessed that it still served, as it did during her childhood, as a meeting place for people who loved fishing . . . and the island. For a moment, she considered pointing the place out to Jonas, then decided against it. What if he pulled an act like the one he had pulled on Big Jake's dock and told all the Tuna Club regulars that she was an outstanding fisherwoman?

A few paces past the Tuna Club, she stopped along the railing and pointed down at the dark brown rocks in the water.

"Down there," she said. "That's where we'll find the crabs, if they're around."

Jonas peered into the depths. "I don't see anything," he said, sounding doubtful.

"They're just about the same color as the rocks, so you have to look carefully." She spoke with the voice of authority. "You go down here and look for them. I'm going to try a bit further along the shore."

Jonas eyed her suspiciously. "You aren't ditching me, are you?"

Cat placed hands on hips and pretended to consider this. "It's a thought." His face fell. "Then again, it's hard to find a man these days who's classy enough to give a girl raw meat. I may just have to hang on to you for a while."

"Really?" Jonas sounded hopeful. He took a step closer, reaching up to play with a strand of hair that had become untucked from behind her ear. "Is that a promise?" His eyes caught and held hers.

Catherine stood motionless beneath his searching look and tried to catch her breath. What was going on? She'd made it clear that this was a truce, nothing more. It was a game. They were pretending to be friends, just for the day. So why was Jonas looking at her as if it was something more? She opened her mouth to speak—Jonas's eyes questioning as he waited to hear her response.

"Just a pinch," she said breathlessly.

"What?"

"The meat. Don't give them very much. Just a little pinch between your thumb and finger. That's all the crabs need."

"A . . . pinch," Jonas repeated, blinking for a moment as if the words had no meaning to him. "I see."

Catherine made her escape, picking her way down the shoreline to another group of rocks along the water. There she peered into the tide pools with what she hoped Jonas would take to be genuine interest. It would not do for him to know she needed to get away from him in order to think.

Not that it was helping. Her thoughts came to her in swirling fragments. What was she doing here? In Catalina. With *him?*

Just this morning, her world had been completely in order. It was true that Daphne's disappearance had wreaked havoc with her emotions. But even in that situation, Catherine knew how to respond. She knew what had to be done—or, at the very least, what she was capable of doing. It was clear what her coping skills were, what came naturally to her. As she had always done before, Cat had followed her instincts.

And now, just hours later, she was still doing what came naturally. The problem was, her instincts were now leading her to run not *from* Jonas, but *to* him. What was happening to her? Should she follow the leading of her mind, which still told her to run as far from him as possible? Or should she listen to her heart, which was urging her to reach out for Jonas's hand and never let go?

I'm definitely delusional. Must be heatstroke.

"Hey, I think I've got one!" Jonas turned a joyous face toward Cat. Even from several feet away, she could read the excitement in his boyish expression. Truly, he loved life. He was much like her mother in that way. Catherine found herself wishing that Anna Salinger had lived long enough to meet him. If she were still alive today, what would she have said to Cat about Daphne? About her entire life? And particularly about Jonas?

It was a question Cat had stopped asking long ago, considering it a painful exercise in futility. But today she asked it, and she didn't have to think long about the answer. Her mother would have loved Jonas. His approach to life was perfectly in sync with hers. "Seize the day," she had been fond of saying. And Jonas Riley, now as much as ever, apparently made a practice of seizing the day on a regular basis—with both hands.

Now if only she could keep him from seizing her in the same way!

Catherine watched as he bent ever closer to the water's surface, balancing with one arm as he reached out with the other to offer up a tiny hamburger peace offering.

"Be careful you don't fall in," she said in her most motherly tone.

Jonas waved away the warning. "Aw, don't worry so much. Come take a look at this." He appeared to be quite pleased with his discovery. "Come here, little crab. I'm not gonna hurt you. Of course, this *hamburger* might clog your arteries and give you *E. coli,* but Cat here doesn't seem to be worried about such things, so I don't think you have reason to be—"

Though he had been careful to keep out of the surf, the stones surrounding the path were slick with ocean water and algae. Before he knew what was happening, his moccasins had slipped on the slimy rocks. "Jonas!" Catherine cried out.

But it was too late.

An hour later—after a visit to both the Metropole Marketplace and the El Encanto Marketplace—Jonas was once again dry from head to toe, clad in a fresh pair of chinos, casual loafers, leather belt, and a short-sleeved Latin-style dress shirt in bold colors.

Catherine remembered that she had once shopped in Avalon with her mother. But few details of those memories remained in her mind, and as a result she was greatly surprised at the selection of stores available. They wandered from shop to shop—Jonas dripping all the while—as Catherine exclaimed over first one discovery, then another. Several times she was tempted to buy an outfit for herself, particularly at one small boutique that featured imported clothing from Mexico. But she managed to refrain, telling herself she had all the vacation wear she'd ever need at home. Jonas, on the other hand, made his purchases cheerfully and seemed to consider the need to do so a tribute to his manly, explorer's spirit.

After Jonas was once again presentable and after she had checked in once with Robin, Catherine felt her thoughts turning to the growling of her stomach. During their search for clothes, they had passed countless eateries that offered everything from hot dogs and tacos to shrimp cocktails and eggplant parmigiana.

"What's next on the agenda?" Jonas asked, sounding even more cheerful now that he was no longer waterlogged.

"Food," Cat told him firmly. "If you don't feed me—and I mean *soon*—I'm not going to be worth anything for the rest of the day."

"Thanks for the warning." He glanced back over his shoulder at the group of restaurants they had just passed. Catherine did the same. "I think I saw a couple of places back there that looked good. Maybe we could—"

But Cat was no longer listening to him. She had frozen in place like a cat who had spied its prey. Though the object of her attention was more than thirty feet away, she had recognized the unmistakable color and style of her sister's hair. "Daphne!"

"What?" Jonas's head snapped back around as he turned to look at her. "Sorry? What about her?"

Catherine ignored the question and began walking, quickly, toward the outdoor patio where she had spotted the runaway bride. The street between her and Daphne was crowded, particularly outside the small café where her sister sat with her back to Catherine. But Cat was certain of what she had seen.

As she drew near, she looked around for any sign of Elliott, but did not know exactly what she was looking for. The tables were crowded so closely together that it was impossible to tell whether Daphne sat at the one behind or in front of her. Several men were seated nearby, and any one of them could be Elliott. Cat would have to speak quickly, in order to get out what she had to say before the young man interrupted.

Or before his older brother did.

Sensing, rather than seeing or hearing, that Jonas was close at her heels, Catherine picked up her pace, beginning to trot, then run. She was just ten feet away from the table when her sister turned and Cat was able to get her first full glimpse of . . .

"*Lucy.*" Her face clouded over with disappointment.

Lucy's eyes flickered upward. "Cat. Try to control your enthusiasm."

165

"Sorry." Catherine dropped into an empty seat at the table, her cheeks flushing hot as the full extent of her embarrassment caught up with her. "I thought you were Daphne. I thought . . . I thought maybe I had been right all along, and that she and Elliott really were here on the island."

Cat felt Jonas's strong hand settle on the tense muscles of her shoulder. She cringed, fearing how ridiculous she must have appeared. "I'm sorry," he said. "I heard what you just said. I don't blame you. You've probably been half-looking for Daphne all day, haven't you?"

Catherine nodded feebly.

"And I haven't done a single thing to make it easier." He continued to speak calmly. Only the twitching of his jaw muscle revealed a sign of the frustration he kept hidden within.

At just that moment, Felicia emerged from the café carrying a tray with two tall glasses of lemonade, a large Caesar salad, and a fresh vegetable sandwich.

"Hey, look who's here! What are you guys up to?"

"Still looking for Daphne," Lucy said disapprovingly. She pointed one finger at Catherine. "I thought we told you to relax. You were supposed to have fun today."

"I *am* having fun!" Cat insisted.

"Really?" Jonas asked eagerly.

"Don't push it," she chided. Three disbelieving faces stared back at her. "Oh, all right. At least I *was* having fun until a few minutes ago. It's not my fault that you and Daph have the same haircut. You live together, for goodness' sake. Don't you think that's a bit much?"

"Mine's longer," Lucy said unapologetically and reached for the Caesar salad.

"Want to join us?" Fee offered.

Catherine turned to Jonas and lifted one eyebrow. But before either of them could respond, Lucy announced,

166

"Nope. They have to keep moving on."

"Actually, we *were* going to get some lunch," Cat informed her.

"Good." One hand waved them away. "Go get some."

"But—"

"*Go* already."

Catherine folded her arms and looked at Lucy with one eyebrow cocked. "Are you this pushy with your clients?"

"Only when they force me to be. Good-*bye*," Lucy said in a saccharine voice that managed to sound anything but sweet.

Jonas shrugged. "I guess that's our answer," he told Cat seriously. "Looks like you and I need to find another restaurant." He grabbed Cat firmly by the hand and began dragging her away.

"Well . . . 'bye again," Felicia said as the two set out back down the boardwalk. The bewildered look she gave Catherine made it clear that she had no idea what was going on.

But then again, thought Cat, neither did she.

As it turned out, Cat and Jonas did not eat at a café that afternoon at all. After much discussion, they decided instead to purchase groceries and supplies at the local market, then cook their lunch on the barbecue pits that were available to visitors, free of charge, out on the mole.

At first, Jonas had resisted, proclaiming there was nothing appetizing about eating on a "mole." But Catherine quickly explained that the mole was simply a man-made breakwater set up in the ocean to the south of Pleasure Pier. And so they dined on juicy, barbecue-style chicken, foil-wrapped ears of corn, and homemade berry cobbler purchased from a bakery down on Sumner Avenue.

"That was perfect," Jonas said, sitting back and patting his stomach at long last. "I seemed to remember you are a good cook."

Catherine brandished the bone of the chicken leg she had just finished polishing off. "Watch it, mister. The man who gets me is going to get an awful lot more than just a good cook. I have brains and talent too."

Jonas inclined his head ever so slightly. "And beauty."

"And beauty?" This mollified her.

"That's what I said."

"Well . . . thank you."

Jonas faked an exaggerated look of concern. "I'm sorry. Was that another lecherous comment?"

"Mmm . . . I'll allow it this one time." Playfully she poked one of his toes with her foot. "You know, Jonas," she said, "I have to confess that I'm actually glad you tricked me into spending the day with you." To her surprise, it did not feel threatening to admit this to him, even though it seemed like it should. Perhaps she was getting used to being around him again.

Or perhaps he had drugged her drink. She pondered this possibility.

"Tell me why you're glad."

Cat moved her foot away from him and began to draw in the dirt with her toes. "I don't know how to put it into words really." Somehow she managed to avoid his gaze. "I guess it just reminds me of the way things used to be. Makes me feel young again. I feel like I don't have a care in the world, even though I know I really do."

"Yeah." Jonas laughed awkwardly. "I noticed how relaxed you were back when we ran into Lucy and Felicia."

Catherine squirmed. "That was different. I got a little carried away."

"Cat." He stared at her until she met his eyes. "You're still worried about your sister."

"I never said I wasn't."

"I want you to trust me," Jonas urged.

"I know you do. I want that too." Catherine stared at her hands. "I'm just not sure I can."

"Is it because I 'tricked' you this morning, like you said?"

"You did do that, didn't you? But no. I knew what you were doing, and I played along because I . . ." Her voice trailed off.

"Because you . . . ?" Jonas prompted. His eyes searched hers as he sought an answer to his question.

"Because . . . because I wanted to spend the day with you, *that's* why." Spoken by another woman, the words could have been an endearment, but Cat flung them at him like a weapon. "*There.* Is that what you wanted to hear?"

"As a matter of fact, it is." Unfazed by her prickly response, Jonas gave her a look that seemed to see right through her. "Look, Cat," he said. "I know you're doing your best. This is really a stretch for you, isn't it—just being here with me?"

She looked at him uncomfortably but said nothing.

"And I know I'm not helping matters any by acting like a schoolboy with a crush, but—" Jonas weighed his words, then started again, this time taking a different approach. "There are so many things I want to tell you . . . about me, about my family," he continued. His voice grew strained and his manner agitated. "About what happened between us all those years ago, and about what's going on inside me now. But I don't want to rush this, Cat. I don't want to rush *you*. I'm beginning to think this is enough change for one afternoon. But I'd like to talk more about us later—"

Catherine stared at him. "*Us?*" She'd been struggling with her feelings all day. But up until this point, she hadn't allowed herself to consider there was even an 'us' to talk about. The feelings of fear she'd been fighting to keep down began to well back up.

"—but for now, I think I'd like it best if we could just *be*. Would that be all right with you?"

A sense of relief flooded over her. Catherine did not know what was going on between them, nor did she know how to respond to him. But for now, she didn't have to know those things. What he was offering now was, in a manner, a reprieve.

The sense of emotional claustrophobia that had overwhelmed her began to recede. If Jonas had pushed, forcing her then to talk about the future of their relationship, she would have been unable to respond. Forced into a choice, she would have been unable to give him what he—and she herself —wanted most: an honest assessment of her feelings. What he offered now was a gift: the gift of time, and of an opportunity to discover what was in her heart.

"Yes, Jonas. Just 'being' would be *perfect* with me," she said thankfully. She longed to reach out to him—to squeeze his hand in gratitude. Instead, she bent down to pick up the remains of their picnic.

"Great." Jonas moved to help her, stuffing bits of cooked chicken and plastic wrap into their used grocery bag. When the area was clean, he gave her a smile that rivaled the sun's ability to warm her, cocked his head in the direction of the boardwalk, and said, "Come on, friend. There's a whole big, beautiful day ahead of us." Though he did not touch her, Cat felt closer to him at that moment than she would have thought possible.

"And," he said easily, "you're stuck with me, so you might as well like it."

So help me, Catherine thought to herself, *I do.*

TEN

It was the first time in more years than she cared to count that Catherine allowed herself to "go with the flow" of events as they swept her along. And they—or rather, Jonas—did, indeed, sweep her . . . entirely off her feet.

Shortly after their picnic lunch, their Catalina adventure began in earnest. Tired now of playing "follower" to Cat's "leader," Jonas picked up a tourist brochure in order to determine where they should head next. As he read, Catherine leaned her back against a brick building whose walls had been warmed by the early afternoon sun. She wondered what Jonas would pick. Snorkeling? Sailing? Hiking up to the Catalina Stables or Botanical Garden?

Every possibility sounded too strenuous for her—especially considering their agreement to just *be*. For weeks—for *months*, ever since her father died—she'd been running around like a madwoman at work. Now that she had finally gotten away from the rat race, she wanted to do something peaceful that would allow her to relax. At the same time, Cat wanted Jonas to enjoy his first trip to the island. During her early childhood, she'd enjoyed all those activities that she now suspected he wished to partake of. She hated to ruin his opportunity to do the same.

She stretched lazily, enjoying the day's heat as it touched her skin. Absently she reached into her bag, pulled out the bottle of the SPF-45 lotion she'd slathered on earlier that morning, and began to apply a second coat. Jonas slipped the

171

pamphlet he had been studying to the rear of the stack in his hands and began to peruse another while, all around him, crowds of day-trippers swarmed the sidewalk.

"It says here there's a self-guided walking tour around town. Interested?"

Catherine drew her sunglasses down on her nose and eyed him curiously from over the top of them. "Are you kidding? No golf? No tennis?"

"Not now. You said earlier you just wanted to get reacclimated. So let's do that. This walk sounds great."

So he really was listening. The revelation pleased her deeply.

"You really are full of surprises, aren't you?" Catherine felt a bit awed.

Jonas wiggled his eyebrows mischievously. "Sweetheart, you don't know the half of it." Cat giggled. The sound seemed strange in her own ears. She was an intelligent, professional woman. It was hard to think of herself as a giggler. But there she was, giggling away like a schoolgirl. And for the life of her, doing so felt like the most natural thing in the world.

Jonas was quick to notice her transformation. "You know, it suits you."

She could sense a compliment coming, but did not mind it. "What suits me?"

"Smiles. Laughter. This whole, new relaxed attitude you've got going. It's quite becoming."

"Thanks, I think." Catherine was not certain the comment was meant entirely as a compliment, but she decided to take it as one. "Where do we begin?"

Jonas consulted his map. "Up Whittley Avenue."

They were already a bit north of Pleasure Pier and so did not have far to go to get to their starting point.

"Then let's go."

Avalon's terrain was exactly as she remembered it. While the streets surrounding Chuck's bed-and-breakfast had been located in the "flats" southwest of Pleasure Pier, the part of town where they were headed was much more hilly. Whittley was steep and curved quickly around to the right. At first they passed small houses, then a Spanish-style church and a red-tile roofed house that, like Chuck's, had been transformed into a bed-and-breakfast.

"This says that house was built by a count," Jonas remarked.

"So was the church," Cat told him. "And see those apartments over there? He used to have stables there that looked out over the bay."

As they continued up the steep hill, Cat could feel the exertion in her lungs and legs. Though she exercised on a regular basis, the walk—or, rather, the *hike*—was giving her body a good workout, and yet Jonas hardly seemed short of breath.

At the top, she spied an arbor made of white wooden trellis work. "Look!" she said excitedly. "There's the pergola." But Jonas had already spied it. Like a man on a mission, he climbed resolutely up the dirt path toward the structure, stopping at the top of the hill to drink in the breathtaking view of Avalon and the bay below them.

Seconds later, Catherine was at his side. Without thinking, she leaned against him—as much for support for her exhausted body as for companionship. In a gesture that seemed both easy and natural, Jonas draped an arm about her shoulders and let it casually rest there.

"It feels so peaceful here," she said quietly. And indeed it did. Despite the crowds below, they had for a moment found a place that was theirs alone.

"I wish I could feel like this more often." The words

slipped out of her before she could weigh or measure them.

"What's stopping you?" There was no judgment to his tone, just compassion and curiosity.

"Well, nothing except . . . me, I guess." In this place, among people who were not a part of her everyday life—including the man who now held her close—the confession was given freely. "I seem to make things harder on myself than they have to be. You may not have noticed, but I'm not always the easiest person in the world to get along with." She laughed lightly. "I know that's hard to believe, but—"

"Tell me what that's like for you," he said, interrupting. His question unnerved her. She was used to being the target of her sisters' accusations. If only he had told her she was right, that she *was* difficult to deal with. Then she would be able to revert to her accustomed defensiveness, to tell him why she had to be the way she was—why her sisters needed her. Why *everything* depended on her keeping a cool head and taking care of business.

Instead, he had simply asked what it was like to be in her shoes. Cat wasn't sure if this was a comfort or a new type of torture she had never encountered before.

"It's . . . hard. And it's also very—" Her eyes flickered to his face, but he was still staring out toward the sea. Catherine let out a deep breath. "It's also very lonely."

Jonas looked at her then and nodded but did not say a word.

It was Catherine's turn to focus on the stirring of the waves in the distance. "I know I must seem like a—what is it you called me the other day? An 'imperious control freak'?"

Jonas made a face at her. "I'm sorry. I never should have said that," he said, his voice filled with regret.

"No. It's okay, really. I mean, I wasn't exactly thrilled at the time," she laughed. "But there's some truth to what you said. I do want to be in control most of the time. It's not that I'm *trying* to be a jerk—"

"Catherine. Nobody ever accused you of that. Your sisters know you love them."

She nodded. "I know they do. But maybe having good motives isn't enough. Do you think Hitler sat around thinking, 'Hmm. What crimes against humanity can I commit today?' No way. He was probably thinking, 'Oh, I'm such a good leader. Look at all I'm doing for my country. I'm making it strong; I'm making it rich. Look at what I'm doing for my race.' Maybe he did have a good motive or two in there somewhere, though it's hard to imagine *where*. But, my word, Jonas. Look at how all his *terrible* motives—hatred, greed, selfishness, and yes, *a need to control*—destroyed the lives of millions."

"Catherine." Jonas slipped his arm off her shoulders then and turned her to face him. "I'm not sure I like this analogy. You're not Hitler. You're not anything like Hitler."

"How about Stalin?"

"Not a chance. You're nothing like them, Cat."

"Yes, I am," she said heavily. "I'm a control freak. You said so yourself."

"Oh, *honey*." Catherine's heart leapt at the sound of the endearment, but she could not allow herself to be comforted. Jonas pulled her into his arms and she stiffly allowed herself to lay her head against his chest. "So dramatic, aren't you? There's no need to be extreme. You're not perfect; I think we've determined that. If not, I'm sure your sisters would testify to that fact." Cat smiled weakly, in spite of the tears that had risen to her eyes. "But you're not a murderous dictator either. Okay?" She nodded mutely against the soft fabric of his shirt. "You're a flesh-and-blood woman with good qualities and bad ones. And just like the rest of us, you have to learn to control the behavior you don't like. There's nothing you can do, except do the best you can and ask God to help you along the way."

That settled it. Jonas really *was* the man Anna would have dreamed of for her daughter—a man who wasn't afraid to talk about God.

Funny how the memories of her mother kept coming back so strongly now. Catherine was remembering how her mother had sat beside her bed, reading Bible stories, talking to her about God. Knowing that her time on earth would be short, Anna Salinger had talked with her children at length about putting their faith in Jesus Christ and living life committed to him. To her two older daughters, who eagerly adopted her faith as their own, she had given the responsibility of teaching the younger ones after she was gone. And obediently, Catherine had done so. It had not been difficult: Even though Lucy and Daphne were only five and three at the time, Anna had already instilled in them a foundation of faith that was easy to build upon in the years that followed.

Catherine sighed. Back then her faith had felt so strong, so real, so alive. It had helped her through so much. And yet, through the years—and particularly since she entered college and broke up with Jonas—it seemed to have grown tired and stiff—more of an adherence to commandments than a relationship with a living God.

"I do ask God for help . . . sometimes," she now admitted. "But I'm not always sure he's giving it to me. And then I eventually stop turning to him at all."

Again, there was no judgment, no accusation of "How can you possibly doubt God?" Jonas just pulled her a little closer and asked, very simply: "What kind of help do you want from

God, Cat? If you could ask him for anything, what would it be?"

This startled her. For so long, she'd felt she had no right to ask God anything . . . and no real confidence that God would answer if she did. She tried to think, but it was hard to get past the sinking feeling that she had failed God in some unforgivable way and had no right to do anything but accept the hand he dealt her.

"I don't know. I feel uncomfortable even thinking about it." She squirmed in Jonas's arms, but he continued to hold her tight.

"Come on, Catherine. Think about it. What do you want from God?"

"I . . . don't know." She tried to wrack her brain. What had she ever wanted from God during the times she actually had turned to him? Images of her mother in her sickbed flashed into Cat's mind, followed by that of Jonas's angry expression when she broke up with him and her father's terrifying paleness as he lay on the conference-room floor.

"I guess I just want . . . want him to make everything all right."

"What do you mean?" Jonas sounded puzzled.

"I don't know. Just—" Catherine lifted her head as the sounds of another group of tourists came rising up over the knoll. "I don't know. That's all. Come on." Though her every instinct resisted, she managed to pull herself from Jonas's embrace. "We should get going. I've got my breath back."

"I don't know that I have," he said grumpily, but reluctantly released her.

Following the instructions in their pamphlet, they followed the curve of East Whittley and turned into Marilla, their moods gradually lightening as they headed back toward town. Taking a side trip down Hiawatha, they found the historic Barlow House where, they learned from the pamphlet, a circus group known as the Travillo Brothers had lived after coming to Catalina to find trainable seals to add to their act. Catherine and Jonas laughed upon learning that it was in the front yard of this home that the family taught their seals how to bounce balls on their noses.

"Now *that* would have been worth walking to see," Jonas said.

"So's the next thing. Keep walking," Catherine ordered.

Once they reached Crescent, they headed southeast, back toward the mole where they had picnicked earlier.

"That's it," Catherine cried, pointing to a structure in the distance. Holly Hill House. Vaguely she remembered her mother's stories regarding the incredible white mansion with its distinctive cupola. She continued to walk, her hand on Jonas's arm to guide him so he could read and walk at the same time.

" 'Built in the late 1800s,' " Jonas quoted, " 'Holly Hill House was the home of engineer Peter Gano, who designed the first freshwater system to service Avalon. Throughout the process of building the system, which ran from Avalon Canyon Springs to the Metropole Hotel, Gano worked with a retired circus horse that was trained to respond to his whistle command. Through this method the horse, named Mercury, walked downhill pulling ropes that were wound around pulleys. These in turn powered a loaded cable car that traveled uphill to where the water system was being laid.' " Jonas let out a long, slow whistle. "That's one talented horse."

"I wonder if the Travillo Brothers' trained sea lions ever performed a public service like that?" Catherine gazed up at the breathtaking home with its circular, open-air cupola patio topped with a coned-shaped roof.

"The story is," Jonas told her, his eyes still on the tourist pamphlet, "that Gano built this place for a woman he loved. But she refused to leave the mainland to live on an island. I guess it was pretty unpopulated back then, and she didn't want to give up her social activities."

"I could give up a lot of social activities for a house like that," Catherine said wryly. She threw Jonas a sidelong glance. "Provided, of course, that the right man lived there."

Jonas grinned gleefully. "There you go, flirting again."

She shrugged. "Whatever. Think what you want."

"Hmph. *Women*." Jonas shook his head. "Apparently our friend Mr. Gano was confused by your gender too. It says here his ladylove made him choose between her and the house. He figured she'd change her mind, so he picked the house. After that, she married another man, and Gano spent the rest of his life living in the house he built for her, which he posted with signs saying, 'No Women Allowed.'"

"That's horrible!"

"I'll say. How could a guy live without women?"

"I'm *serious*," Cat said sorrowfully. "It's so sad. I'd forgotten how terrible it was. Just think of it, Jonas! If he'd known how things were going to turn out, maybe he would have picked differently. His whole life would have gone an entirely different direction. Maybe he'd have had children. Grandchildren. Certainly, he would have had *her*. He must have spent the rest of his days wishing he could go back and choose all over again."

Or maybe he just shut down emotionally, trying to forget about his lost love. Maybe he cut himself off from everyone except his closest family members. I wonder if he became a control freak like me? Or maybe he just cut people out of his life completely. Is that what I'm going to be like someday? Living alone in a beautiful old house that people admire, but without anyone to hold my hand or sit with me on the porch at night? Without any children or grand-

179

children to love and to cherish . . .

"Come on, Cat," Jonas said, interrupting her reverie. "This is getting just a little too depressing for me. Let's head back to the boardwalk and get a snow cone."

And that's exactly what they did. Afterward, not content to settle for a simple walking tour, Jonas insisted that they finish off their day with some other type of physical activity. Cat was in favor of horseback riding but was not dressed appropriately. Jonas was a skilled golfer and tennis player but refused to spend his time on an activity he could engage in back home. In the end, they chose to rent a rowboat and take it out on the bay, where several children also paddled about in the gentle waves.

It was late in the afternoon before Catherine finally began to think about going back to the mainland. "I guess we should probably grab something quick to eat before heading home?" She tried to keep the words light, but they came out sounding dull and dispassionate.

"Maybe." Jonas gave her a quick wink that made her heart flutter. "Or we could make the reservations now and then have a nice, leisurely dinner before we actually leave."

Catherine turned woeful eyes on her dirt-covered linen pants and shirt. "Uh . . . define 'leisurely,' " she said ruefully. "I'm afraid I can't go anyplace too fancy. They'd throw me out."

"You look fine," Jonas assured her.

"No," Cat corrected him. "*You* look fine. I look like I've been in an earthquake." His chinos and Latin-style shirt had, as a matter of fact, held up well under the day's events. Even his newly purchased loafers, which were not exactly made for heavy-duty walking, had served him well. Catherine's lighter clothing, however, now clung dingily to her sticky, sun-screen-slathered skin.

"Well, you look fine to me," he assured her. "But I don't want to make you feel uncomfortable. Don't give it another thought." He glanced at his watch. "There is, however, one quick errand I have to do. Do you mind if I excuse myself for just a few minutes? I promise I won't leave you waiting long."

"Don't be silly. Do what you have to do. I'll wait for you over there by the dive shop."

"Thanks. You're a doll." Before Catherine realized what was happening, he had leaned forward and pressed his lips to her forehead in the gentlest of kisses.

Then he was gone.

Cat's heart raced. Her face felt warm where he had touched her, and she could still feel the pressure of his skin against hers.

What was that?

What was he up to, anyway? Jonas had said he had just wanted to *be*. But what was he *be*-ing, anyway?

She tried to make sense of Jonas's behavior during the day. He wasn't exactly courting her; in fact, he'd pulled back from any such declaration. But he treated her like a girlfriend. Not a new girlfriend, but an old one he felt safe with. Which, in a way, she was. But the difference was, he was acting as if she were his *current* girlfriend, as if they shared experiences that made them feel safe with one another.

And that wasn't right. She *wasn't* his girlfriend; in fact, they were just barely friends. She had no idea how she would feel toward Jonas—or he toward her—once they returned to the real world and all the problems it held. Somehow, Avalon's magic had enveloped them. No doubt the spell would be broken, and she and Jonas would go back to what they had been until that morning: professional rivals and verbal sparring partners.

Catherine waited for Jonas for five minutes, then ten, then

decided to make use of her time by calling the office once more before the five o'clock mass exodus she was sure would occur in her absence. Carol Kincaid answered the phone, explaining that Robin had a doctor's appointment.

"I insisted that the poor thing go home after that," added the temp. "She was exhausted. And everything's quiet here. Robin said it was the slowest week we've had all year, which is a good thing, considering you and your sister are both on vacation."

Catherine blinked. She opened her mouth to tell the temp that she most certainly was *not* on vacation, then closed her mouth again. What did it matter? She'd be back in a day or two anyway. And it was good to know the office was running smoothly and that Carol Kincaid was handling things well. It seemed, in fact, that everything was running just fine without her. She was surprised to realize she didn't mind all that much.

"Well, then, thank you, Carol. I'll check back in tomorrow —if I'm not back by then." Thoughtfully she turned off the cell phone and stowed it in her purse.

Another ten minutes, and Jonas still was not back. Now Cat began to worry. Had something happened to him? Had he thought better of the kiss and been forced to assume a new identity? A slight feeling of panic had set in by the time he finally appeared. Cat noticed right away that he was carrying a large bag and looking quite pleased with himself.

"Look at you, you little shopaholic," she teased. "A little emergency patronage, I see?"

"Exactly." Jonas presented her with the bag. "For you."

"For . . . me?" She stared at him, not understanding. "What for?"

"Open it. You'll see."

"But—"

"Stubborn woman. *Open* it, or I'll open it for you."

Reluctantly at first, and then with a growing sense of excitement, Catherine reached into the bag and pulled away the tissue paper that surrounded her gift.

"Oh, Jonas!" she exclaimed, and pulled from the bag a simple white peasant blouse and brightly colored skirt of soft, crinkly cotton.

"There. Now you have no excuse. You *must* have dinner with me."

"But I can't accept this!"

"Why not?"

Catherine looked at him with teary eyes that begged him to understand. *Because then I'll feel beholden to you. No matter what you ask, I'll do. Even if that means letting Daphne go . . . or letting you back into my life.*

"It's too much, Jonas. I'd feel . . . obligated."

"How about we make a new pact then. Remember what I said about accepting no ultimatums?"

"Ye-es." Catherine remembered him saying something about that.

"Well, now we'll say, 'No strings.' This is a gift, Catherine. It means nothing more than you want it to mean."

Catherine wasn't sure what he meant by that. But so great was her desire to accept his gift that she decided to let the comment pass.

"All right then. You've convinced me. Shall we head to dinner?"

"We shall."

"Where to?"

Jonas patted the back pocket of his pants, which held his faithful pamphlets. "I know just the place. Trust me."

And at that moment, Catherine realized that she did.

★ ★ ★ ★ ★

At Jonas's insistence, they ate at Mi Casita on Clarissa Avenue.

"Just look at us," he said, gesturing toward their Latin-influenced attire. "Where else would we eat? The waffle house?"

"We do look at little like out-of-work salsa dancers, don't we?" Cat agreed. Hours later, at the end of their meal, she agreed that Jonas had made a superb choice. Both food and atmosphere were extraordinary.

"Come on," Jonas said after he had paid. "It's almost time to go home. But first I want to take you on one more little walk."

Catherine followed him back down to the serpentine wall of the waterfront. From there they followed the front street, Crescent, back toward the mole, where the avenue turned into Pebbly Beach Road.

She smiled a slow, secret smile. *Jonas and his tourist brochure.* Cat knew where he was taking her: the sheltered area just before Abalone Point, otherwise known as Lovers Cove. Through it was growing dark, the lights dancing on the water instilled in Catherine a feeling of safety . . . and of celebration. Ahead of them, the crescent moon hung just above Mt. Ada, the 350-foot hill located near the bay. The former Wrigley mansion, built on the slopes of Mt. Ada, gleamed white under the floodlights that shone upon it, making it stand out from the black hillside.

"It's a beautiful night." Cat turned to Jonas with questions in her eyes.

Why had he brought her here?

"It is." Jonas agreed, taking a deep breath of the cool night air. "Romantic."

It was, Cat had to admit, the perfect kind of night for love.

Her thoughts turned to Daphne and Elliott. *Has the same moon, the same stars captured them?* She resisted the impulse to step forward and lean her shoulder against Jonas's strong frame, as she had done earlier that afternoon. *Are they as drawn to one another as I am to Jonas?*

Then a feeling of panic swept through her.

"What are you thinking?" Jonas looked down at her, concern written on his features.

Cat sighed and shook her head. "Daphne. I'm still worried about her. I know you think I'm a meddling old fuddy-duddy. But I care about her, Jonas. I really do."

"I know."

"Maybe I take myself too seriously sometimes. But I'd rather take my responsibilities too seriously than not seriously enough." Though the temperature had not dropped much, Catherine suddenly felt chilled. "Do you know who was the one who lectured Lucy the first night she took a drink at a high school dance? Or the one who had *several* talks with Felicia about what was, and was not, appropriate behavior with boys? Or the one who—" She bit her lip. "The one who still worries about Daphne every time she goes out after work?"

She was shaking a bit now, feeling more than the chill of the night air. Her eyes stung, and Jonas's image began to grow blurry. "I'm too young for this, Jonas." A few tiny hiccups of laughter escaped, and tears began to flow in earnest. "Look at me. I'm becoming hysterical. I'm not even a mother, you know. I'm just a sister with an overinflated sense of self-importance."

Jonas reached out and pulled her into the security of his embrace. "Now you're just being hard on yourself again. You're not a bad guy, remember?" As he spoke, he patted her back in a comforting manner. Gratefully, Cat clung to him, thankful for the support and the opportunity to release the emotions that had been pent up for so long.

"I know you're right. I just can't help feeling like I'm doing something wrong. Like somehow this is my fault. It may be, you know. I tried too hard to make Daphne become what I wanted. I pushed her away—"

"You didn't push her *away*. You just . . . pushed. There's a difference."

"Oh, Jonas." How could he be so forgiving? She was so hard on her sisters. And she'd been so hard on him. "You're sweet. But you *like* me. For some reason I fail to comprehend, you seem to actually *like* me. So I guess you're predisposed to give me the benefit of the doubt. I'm not so sure Daphne will be."

"I guess you'll find out soon enough."

"I guess so," Cat answered glumly. Whenever *that* would be. Friday was just a day and a half away, and she still had no idea where to begin the next phase of her search. Stopping the wedding was probably no longer a possibility. She would just have to wait until Daphne came home and deal with the consequences then. On Tuesday, when she first learned of Daphne's disappearance, Cat had wanted nothing so much as to find and give that girl a piece of her mind. But all she wanted now was the chance to take her sister in her arms, hold her close, and tell her how very sorry she was for hurting her.

"When you see her on Friday, I mean," Jonas continued.

Catherine pulled herself away from the comforting warmth of his shirt. The fabric against her ear must have caused her to misunderstand him. "What?"

With one arm Jonas released her shoulder, reached into his back pocket, and pulled out a wallet. From it, he withdrew an official-looking piece of paper. "This is our itinerary," he said. "We pick the tickets up at the airport." She just stared at him blankly. "I'm taking you to them, Cat," he went on. "Tomorrow morning. We have a 7:00 A.M. flight to St. Lucia."

Cat stared at the paper, made no move to take it from him. "St. Lu—" It took a moment for his words to register. "You can't mean the Caribbean?"

"Do you know of any other St. Lucias?" Cat watched, mesmerized by the round *O* his lips formed in the pronunciation of "*Loo*-shuh." *St. Lucia . . . St. Lucia . . .* Her mind spun. It took a moment before she could think clearly, but then the questions began to flow.

"Have you talked to them? Is everything all right? Are they still going through with the wedding?" She plucked at his sleeve with excitement.

Jonas held up one hand as if to stave off her verbal onslaught. "I haven't talked to Elliott since before they left. I made the decision to buy the tickets yesterday, after you stormed your way into my office. But I didn't know until today whether I was really going to take you or not. I had to know that you weren't going to just go in there screaming and yelling and mess up their wedding."

"You still don't know that I won't."

"No, I don't. But there's one other little thing to consider."

"What's that?"

"Trust."

Trust. He'd been telling her all along that she could trust him. Now he was proving beyond a shadow of a doubt that he believed in her.

"But I can't let you pay for my ticket," she protested.

He shrugged. "It's done."

"Jonas." She gave him the sternest look she could muster. "It's not right. It's not your responsibility. A ticket like this, no advance notice—it must have cost a fortune." She waved it in front of his eyes. "I don't know where on earth those two kids got the money."

"Well, actually—" Jonas looked at her sheepishly. "They got it from me."

"They *what?*"

"Not all of it. It's complicated. I'll explain later. For now, let's just say it's a gift."

"I still don't understand why you—"

Jonas gently placed one finger upon her lips. "Trust."

Cat pushed his hand away firmly and tried again. "But I have to pay you back if I—"

The finger returned. "Trust."

She stepped back, just out of his reach. "But I'm not making any promises. I still don't think this wedding is a good idea." She expected that to change things. But Jonas's expression remained calm. The look he gave her was unwavering.

Catherine raised her pale blue eyes to his confident brown ones. "Trust," she repeated.

The warmth of Jonas's smile chased away the cold.

"By jove," he said, "I think she's got it."

ELEVEN

"All right, Jonas. Time to spill your guts." Catherine turned in her airline seat and gave him a hard look.

"Excuse me?" He gave up trying to fix the tray table attached to the seat in front of him and gave her his full attention.

"You heard me. I've still got a lot of questions for you, mister," she said sternly.

"Wait a minute." Jonas gave her the innocent stare of the wrongly accused. "I thought I was the good guy here. Remember? I'm the benefactor who bought your ticket."

"That's right," Catherine said, jumping on the admission. "And speaking of buying tickets—"

"Ah. I should have guessed it would come to this." Jonas settled back against his seat, getting as comfortable for the flight ahead as his six-foot-one-inch frame would allow. "Fine. Go ahead, Ms. Prosecutor. Your witness."

Catherine's lips twitched. "Thank you." She folded her arms across her chest and began to speak in a strong, accusatory tone. "Mr. Riley, is it a fact that sometime before the twenty-third of July, 1997, you purchased two tickets in the names of Daphne Salinger and Elliott Riley?"

"Objection."

"What?" Cat reverted to her normal speaking voice. "You can't object. You're the witness."

"We have to double up on our roles," Jonas explained logically. "Who's going to be the judge—the pilot?"

Cat rolled her eyes. "There is no judge. This is not a real courtroom."

"I still object."

"On what grounds?"

Jonas raised one eyebrow and gave her a suave, sophisticated wink. "On the grounds that you're far too attractive to be asking me such difficult questions. It's hard for me to concentrate."

Catherine set her lips in a firm, straight line. "I'm afraid I'm going to have to find you in contempt of court."

"Sorry, you can't. It's not a real courtroom, remember?"

"*Jonas.*" She waggled one finger in front of his face. "I'm serious here. I want to know why you paid for Elliott and Daphne's tickets."

Responding to her change in tone, he stopped playing and answered seriously. "I didn't actually."

"But you said you gave them the money."

"I only gave them some of it. Most came from their savings. They thought they had enough to cover everything, but things got complicated."

This didn't sound good. Catherine leaned forward to hear him better over the noise of the airline attendants serving a meal. "Complicated how?"

"At first, they were in pretty good shape," Jonas explained. "I know it sounds expensive to elope to the Caribbean. But actually, this way they only had their own expenses to worry about. Did you know that when you figure in the cost of all the details, the average wedding in the U.S. ends up costing around twenty thousand dollars?"

She looked at him, horrified. "You're making that up. Felicia's wasn't anywhere near that much."

"No. Seriously. It was on the news. Running away was actually the least expensive option. This way, Elliott and

Daphne didn't have to pay for catering, flowers, expensive photography—"

"I get the idea," Cat interrupted. These were not the details she needed. "They're a couple of real penny-pinchers. So where do you come in, Daddy Warbucks?"

Jonas laughed. Catherine loved the way it brought out the sparkle in his eyes. "I'm getting to that. They figured at first that they could zip into the country, get married, and zip out again. That way they'd be home before you even knew they were missing."

It sounded ridiculous. Nutso. Absurd.

And totally Daphne.

"And you actually advocated this plan?" she said disapprovingly.

Jonas refused to become defensive. "Unfortunately for them," he said, ignoring her comment, "visitors have to be residents on the island for two working days before applying for a marriage license. To make matters worse, the application needs to be filed at least four working days before the day of the wedding."

Catherine was unsympathetic. "Not exactly the same as running away to Las Vegas, is it?"

"Not exactly."

"So why didn't they do it that way—someplace local—if they were in such a rush?"

"They had looked around, but eventually made up their mind to go to St. Lucia. I don't blame them; it's a beautiful spot. My parents took us there for a vacation when we were kids, and Elliott wanted to share the romance of it with Daphne." Jonas shook his head admiringly. "I can see why. I can't wait to share it with you."

Cat felt herself blush bright pink from her hairline down to the neckline of her sleeveless denim shirt. Jonas's compliments were becoming more direct with every passing hour.

"Wait'll you see it, Cat," he said, his voice filled with excitement. "Honey-colored beaches . . . stately palm trees . . . and everywhere you turn: oranges, limes, lemons, pineapples . . . mangoes, bananas, plums. When Elliott and I were kids, we used to visit the banana plantations and hike up to waterfalls in the mountains. We poked around the hot mud pools and sulfur vents. And we climbed the Pitons—these volcanic mountains at the southwest end of the island that look like the pyramids. You wouldn't believe all the vegetation in the rain forest—amazing, flame-colored flowers, orchids, and hibiscus everywhere you turn. The place really *is* a honeymooner's dream. So Elliott and Daphne figured that since they didn't have a lot of time anyway, getting away to someplace exotic would at least leave them with the feeling they'd had some time away together."

"Okay. Sounds reasonable." Cat thought about that comment for a moment, then retracted it. "Wait. Let me rephrase that. I *understand* why they wanted to get married there. But that still doesn't explain why *you* had to step in."

"There was no way they could stay there for six full working days or more without financial help," Jonas explained. "And the timing was right, with you giving Daphne almost a full week off. They just needed a little more time and money. That's when I offered to help."

"I can't *believe* you did that."

"Catherine." Jonas lifted her hand from the armrest and began to play idly with her fingers. "Elliott is my brother and I love him. This is what he wanted. Besides, if I hadn't helped out, they would have done what you said. They would have gone to Las Vegas, which wasn't what they wanted at all. Is that what you wish had happened?"

Cat scowled. It wasn't, and Jonas knew it.

"This was their dream," he continued. "Why shouldn't I help them make it come true if it was within my means to do so? They're not teenagers, Cat. It really is up to them what they do, and nothing you or I say could ever change that."

"Well . . . ," she began grudgingly, "I still don't agree that you did the right thing. But I can understand *why* you did it. And at least you're taking me down there so I can see for myself what's going on."

"Provided we can find them," Jonas offered cheerfully.

"What is *that* supposed to mean?"

"Not to worry." Jonas patted her hand benevolently. "I'm not exactly sure which hotel they're staying at. But don't fret about it. I'm sure we can find them. How many honeymoon suites can there be on any one tropical island?"

Try dozens . . .

Catherine's heart sank. "*Ohhhhhh.* Don't say 'honeymoon suite.' I don't want to even think about it. They've already been down there alone together for . . . how many days?"

Jonas dropped the lighthearted tone. "Are you implying that Daphne and Elliott are, uh . . . sharing a room?"

"Well . . ." Cat shrugged. "It would be an awfully big temptation."

"I promise you, there's no way my brother would take advantage of your sister in that way. He *loves* her. He wouldn't do anything to hurt her." He thought about it for a moment. "No, I'm *sure* he'll wait. Now, Daphne . . ."

"You can hold it right there, mister," Cat shot back, but then she didn't have anything more to add. She wanted to believe Jonas was right. But . . . two young adults in love? She knew Daphne had been saving herself for marriage. But now that she was almost there, would she be able to maintain that standard? Impulsive, free-spirited Daphne? "I'd just feel a lot better if I knew where they were."

"I know." Jonas relented. "I was just kidding before. Of *course* I know where they are. I'll take you to their hotel tonight, just as soon as we get into Castries."

Cat breathed a sigh of relief.

"There. Do you feel better?" With strong fingers, Jonas reached over and gently touched her cheek. "I promise you, there's nothing to worry about. My brother has the highest moral standards."

"Well . . ." Cat was not yet fully convinced. "My dad always used to tell us girls that we shouldn't trust men."

"I can understand why he'd say that. He's a dad; he worries. You, more than anyone, should relate to that. Besides, there's some truth to what he said. Some men, like some women, aren't trustworthy. But when you find a good man—one who loves God and follows his commandments—I think it's okay to risk believing in him."

Catherine thought about this for a minute. She was beginning to believe that maybe, just *maybe,* Jonas was exactly the kind of man he had just described. If so, wouldn't it stand to reason that his brother might be too? "So you're telling me that Elliott's a Christian?"

"He is. As am I." He spoke with quiet pride that showed a respect for what he believed in. "And you? What do you believe, Cat?"

"I *believe* in God," she said slowly. "And I became a Christian when I was young. But I haven't been terribly good about acting that way."

"What makes you say that?"

"Oh, I don't know." She glanced around the cabin, thinking. "You always hear preachers talk about how we're supposed to have this wonderful faith in God. To trust him in any situation. But I guess I wasn't ever a very good Christian, because I never had that kind of faith. I was really angry with

God for letting my mother die. I got angry with him again, years later, when I ended up losing you. By the time Dad died, I guess I was even past being angry. I mean, I still go to church and all. But it's been a long time since I really expected God to make a difference in my life."

Jonas nodded. Then, taking her hand in his, he leaned back against the seat to think. They sat hand in hand, breathing recirculated oxygen and thinking about the past. After a while, Jonas turned to her again and asked, "Do you remember what we talked about at the docks the other day?" Cat nodded. "You said that my father let your family down when he double-crossed your dad. I wondered then if you felt that your mom and dad, too, had let you down—you know, your mom died and your dad just . . . wasn't all there?"

"I remember," Catherine said quietly.

"Well . . . ," Jonas began slowly. "What about God, Cat? Did you feel that he failed you too?"

The look she gave him was one of shock. "Don't say that!"

"Why not?" he said, sounding surprised at the urgency in her tone.

"It's . . . it's—"

"You look scared." His eyebrows furrowed in an expression of concern. "Are you afraid something's going to happen to you if you question God?"

"*He* didn't fail me, Jonas," she said anxiously. "It isn't possible. He's God. If anyone failed, it's me. I mean, look at my track record. I've alienated all my sisters. I turned my back on you twelve years ago after you wouldn't prove your love to me the way I wanted you to. And I—"

"What else did you do, Cat?"

Catherine forced the words to her lips. "I turned my back on God! I was mad at him, and I doubted him, and I stopped going to him. The only times I pray anymore are when I want something, or I can't think of anything else to do. God must hate that. I'll bet he feels used."

"Well, I'm not God, so I can't really say," Jonas told her simply. "But I really don't think he feels that way. I think it just makes him really happy when you pray, no matter what your reason is for doing it. He wants to meet your needs. He wants to hear your heart. What could you be saying that he would possibly hate?"

"That I want something—again."

"Well, sure you do. He knows that. Don't you think he knows that whether you tell him so or not? You're not going to be able to stop wanting things, Cat. All you've done is stop going to him with your feelings about those desires. You're not hiding a thing."

Cat just stared at him. Jonas sounded so incredibly forgiving, and she wanted desperately to believe that God could be too. "But . . . it just feels wrong to go to him, all sweet and nice, when I'm praying, and then to feel all this frustration and anger when I don't understand why my prayers aren't answered."

"Don't fake being sweet and nice then. Just be you."

Catherine made a face at him. "Thanks a lot."

"You know what I mean, Cat. Don't fake your emotions with God. When you're angry, tell him so. When you're confused or frustrated, share those emotions with him."

It sounded so simple when Jonas said it that way.

"And when you're standing by the ocean's edge, feeling overwhelmed by the majesty of God's creation . . ." He sounded genuinely moved, even as he spoke. ". . . or when you're tucked into your bed at night, feeling warm and cozy and thankful for all the blessings in your life, then praise him. It's important that you share with God the way you feel about him, Cat. But you're not going to feel anything—good *or* bad—if you don't spend time with him."

"I'm guess I'm afraid to do that," she admitted.

"Why?"

"Because he . . . he sees me."

"And what does he see?"

Catherine felt her face crumble into tears. "He sees the *real* me, Jonas. The me you don't seem to see. I know you think I'm wonderful. I don't know why, but it seems like you do. You haven't seen the *real* me though. The bad me. I'm controlling, like you said. But there's more to it than that. I'm stubborn. I'm self-righteous. I always have to win. I believe the worst about people. And I have no faith—"

"And how do you think God feels about that? How does he feel toward *you*, Cat?"

"He must just *hate* me!" she cried. "I feel so ashamed to go to him. Why can't I just believe? Why can't I just have faith?"

"Oh, Catherine." There was a catch in his voice, and he pulled her close. "Don't you know how precious you are to God? How deeply, how passionately he feels toward you?"

Catherine knew the people all around them could hear her crying, but she didn't care. She just turned her head and sobbed into his shirt.

"Sweetheart, it says so right in the Bible," Jonas told her. "It's not just a book of rules. It's a love story. It's all about how much he loves *you*." His lips pressed gently against the soft skin at her right temple. "All this time we've been talking about trust. I've tried to show you that you can trust me. But I'm a human being, just like you are. I'm full of flaws and very capable of failing you—even though I don't mean to.

"It's a whole different thing with God though." Jonas's voice was filled with confidence. "He's not going to fail you; you have to get that through your head. He may *confuse* you from time to time. And, yes, he'll even let you get angry and frustrated. But he will not fail you. Ever. God doesn't make mistakes. You can trust him with control . . . of your anger about your mom and your dad, of your life . . . of Daphne's. Of *our* relationship."

He gripped her by the shoulders and held her out away from him so he could clearly see her face. "And you also can trust him with your heart."

The reference to her father brought to mind something that had been nagging at her for days. "It was really strange to see your dad again after all these years," she said, and began to sniffle. "Lucy said Daphne thought he'd been to see my father."

"You didn't know that?" Jonas handed her a white linen handkerchief, drawn from his pocket.

"No. Daddy never said anything. Do you know what happened?"

"My father went to see your father a few weeks before he died," he said. "You see, he has struggled for so long with feelings of guilt over what happened. Those feelings intensified when Elliott and Daphne started dating. He felt that if he was ever going to work this through with his old friend, he'd better go ahead and do it.

"So he went over to your dad's house and asked him for forgiveness. And . . . well, your dad forgave him."

The enormity of the disclosure shook her. "I still can't believe he didn't tell me about this."

"Maybe there just wasn't time. Maybe he never had the chance, never knew how to bring it up."

Catherine sadly considered the very real possibility. "I wish I'd had a chance to talk to him about it. About the whole issue of forgiveness. It was something he struggled with, just like I do."

"That's one thing you can talk to God about," Jonas suggested.

Cat nodded. "I've carried in my heart so much hatred for your father, for so many years," she marveled. "And you know, it just doesn't feel so important, now that I know our fathers made peace. I'm just so sorry, Jonas. I'm sorry I made you choose between me and your father."

"We were young, Catherine," he said quietly. "We were both stupid in our own ways."

"But we might have been happy together!"

"That's true. But we might just as easily have been miserable. We were both immature; we might not have been ready for a relationship. Besides, it won't help us for you to keep beating yourself up about it. God's timing really is best. If he had wanted us together back then, it would have happened."

Cat considered this new bit of information. It was a possibility she hadn't even thought of before. "But . . . twelve years!" she cried. "Think of how painful it was to lose each other."

"Sweetheart." His deep brown eyes were filled with compassion. "Don't you know by now that you never really lost me? You just misplaced me for a while."

His words awakened a sense of longing deep within her. She dared not hope . . . yet could not keep from asking, "What . . . what do you mean?"

Jonas weighed each word carefully. "Catherine, I lost you once before; I have no desire to have that happen again. I want you to trust me. I know you don't yet. But I'm willing to wait . . ."

He paused, looked down at his lap as if searching for words, then tried again. "Ever since Elliott and Daphne started dating, I've been thinking about the way things used to be between you and me and wondering what they would be like if we tried again. I think yesterday was just a taste of how good we are together. I want to give you all the time in the world to figure out how you feel toward me, Cat. But at the same time, I'm going crazy, wanting to know your feelings."

He drew in a deep breath. "I'm not going to ask now. Not here, on a plane. Not while so many things are still up in the air." He grimaced. "No pun intended. I was referring to things with Elliott and Daphne. First, we have to deal with them . . . and we'll do it together. I still think they're old enough and wise enough to make their own decisions. But I think your concerns have merit too. Maybe I'm too lenient, and maybe you're too strict."

A hint of hopefulness crept into his voice. "Maybe that's why we're perfect for each other . . . we balance each other out. But anyway, we'll handle first things first. I know your heart is with your sister right now—"

Catherine blinked at him, her attention fully captured by what he had been saying. *Sister? What sister . . . ?*

"—but the time is coming, Cat, when I'm going to need to have an answer. I'm going to need to know how you feel toward me, whether you could ever see me as something more than . . . well, more than just the guy who helped you find your sister."

If he had asked her in that moment, Catherine would have agreed to follow him to the moon. But he did not. He was giving her time to work out her problems. But would there ever be time enough to deal with all the issues she felt toward him, toward herself, and toward God?

Jonas encircled her fingers with his own and drew her hand to his face. Laying her palm gently against his lips, he kissed it softly.

"Oh, Cat. You look worried. Don't be. Everything's going to be all right. Daphne and Elliott will be fine, no matter what happens. And you and I don't have to figure everything out at once. Think about what I said. Trust God. Talk to him about what's going on inside. He'll take care of both of us. I promise."

The stewardess stopped beside them then with her beverage cart, preventing Jonas from saying more. But by that time, he had already given Catherine more than enough to think about. As Jonas went about wheedling extra peanuts out of the flight attendant, she turned her face to the window and watched the clouds beneath them.

Within twenty-four hours, Davis Pierce would be flying solo at the follow-up meeting with Apollo Athletics, while she would be landing on a tropical island with Jonas Riley. She shook her head. How could so much change in just a few days?

The night before, prior to calling Davis and Leo Randolph at their homes to explain that a family emergency would prevent her from attending the meeting, it had occurred to Catherine that all this still might be an elaborate plan of the Rileys to ruin Salinger & Associates' relationship with Apollo. Hadn't that been her original fear—that Daphne's elopement was nothing more than a cleverly designed scheme masterminded by Jonas Riley? Yet here he was beside her, missing his own scheduled appointment at Apollo, for the sake of both their families.

But what was really amazing, she thought, was the way *she* had changed, the way her priorities had shifted. There had been no question in her mind that she needed to miss the meeting. Family came first. Always.

Leo had been put out with her for missing the meeting. But that was his problem. He could forgive her when she got home . . . or not. He could select their company . . . or go elsewhere for service. It didn't matter to her anymore. She had more important issues to deal with.

She had a relationship with her sister to mend, lines of communication with God to reopen . . .

And a chance at love that could forever change her world.

TWELVE

From the moment she stepped off the tiny prop plane that had carried them to the island, Catherine had only one thing on her mind: finding Daphne.

Or rather, two things. Finding Daphne . . . and juggling a jumble of feelings directed toward the attractive traveling companion who had spent the day carrying her bags.

She was exhausted. Their flight had left LAX at seven that morning. They had changed planes in Dallas and arrived in San Juan at dinnertime. After a two-and-a-half-hour layover, they had boarded the smaller airplane and headed for St. Lucia. Though they had only their carry-on luggage and so were able to avoid baggage claim, it was still close to midnight by the time they arrived at the hotel.

Catherine hadn't expected to care for the resort. She pictured such places as havens for globe-trotting gigolos and spoiled jet-setters. Sometime during their monotonous flight that day, however, Jonas had explained that most of the tropical resorts were quite respectable. In fact, he had learned from Elliott that the Caribbean was becoming a very popular choice among brides and grooms who wished to avoid the fuss—and as he had told her earlier, the expense—of a full-scale stateside wedding.

"It's the perfect vacation: sunny, warm, relaxed. What better way to spend your wedding day?" He sounded sold on the option. "The bigger resorts offer wedding packages and have full-time staff who handle all the details."

"What details?" Cat grumbled. She was tired. She was hungry. She wanted her sister. "I thought eloping was supposed to be so simple?"

"Well, there's the paperwork, for one thing. They handle all the documents, pay the legal fees, hire the minister. Many of them give complimentary announcement cards and a small champagne reception. The bride gets a free facial at the beauty spa and bouquet of tropical flowers. I think Elliott gets a boutonniere too. This place offered them a two-tier wedding cake, but they declined. Daphne said it would just depress her to have no one there to eat it."

The thought bothered Catherine too.

"They'll get a video of the ceremony," Jonas added, "and a handful of photos, I suppose. Afterward, the hotel gives them a romantic, candlelight dinner for two and breakfast in bed the morning after."

"Whew!" Cat let out a long breath. "No wonder they didn't have any money for an extra plane ticket. All that must've cost a fortune."

"Nope. Less than a thousand bucks."

"Seriously?" Catherine was beginning to see the appeal of an island wedding herself. Simple. Inexpensive. And a great place to celebrate future wedding anniversaries. She cast a sidelong glance in Jonas's direction.

They had hailed a cab outside the Virgie airport, just north of the island's capital city of Castries. On the journey from the airport, Catherine had pressed her nose against the window, trying to catch a glimpse of the charming old Caribbean city.

"You won't see much at night," Jonas said, but she'd already discovered that. "Tomorrow, you'll be amazed. There are buildings that I think go back hundreds of years. In many ways, however, the city is quite modern. It's where most of the island's industry, including a big oil plant, is located."

"I guess I'll have to take your word for it." Catherine had continued to stare out the window. It didn't matter. She was in no mood for sightseeing anyway. She wanted only to see her little sister. Seeming to understand this, Jonas fell silent and left her to her thoughts. Several minutes later, they had arrived at the hotel.

As she stepped into the lobby, Cat was greeted by the sound of loud jazz pouring out of the hotel's bar. She stepped immediately to the immense marble counter.

"I need to know the room number for Daphne Salinger," she burst out unceremoniously. "Or Elliott Riley. Either one. It's an emergency."

The man behind the counter seemed unimpressed by her outburst. "I'm sorry. I cannot give out that information."

Cat turned on her heel and gave Jonas a beseeching look.

"Sorry. I don't have the room number," Jonas told her. "I planned all along to fly over for the wedding, but in all the excitement I didn't make any solid arrangements with Elliott. I figured that when I got here, I'd just hang out in the lobby until I found them."

"You're sure this is the right hotel though?"

"Unless they changed their minds. But considering all the work they put into planning this, that's highly unlikely."

Catherine turned back to the darkly tanned, brown-eyed man behind the counter. Though some people look uncomfortable in the formal black tie, pants, and white shirt worn by waiters and hotel service staff, the style suited him and seemed to add to his carefully nurtured "young sophisticate" persona. "Can you at least ring their rooms then?" she inquired.

"Yes ma'am. Of course." He reached for the phone.

She sighed. At least the man wasn't going to play the old "I can't tell you if they're registered here" game. She watched in anticipation as he waited on the line. Finally, he slipped the receiver back into its cradle and gave her a painfully apologetic look. "I am so sorry. There is no answer in either room."

Cat looked at her watch. Five after twelve. She turned to Jonas. "They may already be asleep. At least, I *hope* they're asleep . . ."

"Many people are sleeping," the clerk agreed.

Cat gave him a strange look. *I wasn't talking to* you.

"But then again," the man continued, "also *many* guests choose to take a romantic walk on our beaches at this time of night." He gave her a knowing look.

Catherine's eyes opened wide. *Oh!* He was trying to help. It was against the rules to give her a room number, but he was offering a hint as to where her sister and Elliott had gone.

"Ah!" She slapped her hands back down on the counter and leaned forward eagerly. "That sounds lovely. I don't suppose you could tell which direction is the *most* romantic?"

He shook his head sorrowfully. "That information is, I am afraid, reserved for our privileged guests." The man's voice was dripping with regret.

Cat cocked her head to one side and looked at him quizzically. "But you just said—"

"Catherine." Jonas pulled at her sleeve and whispered in her ear. "I believe he wants us to check in."

"Well, we will, I'm sure. But first, I want to—"

"No," Jonas insisted. "You don't understand. He's not going to take no for an answer. If you don't do what he wants, you'll never find out where Daphne and Elliott went." *So, Jonas figured out what was going on too.*

Cat resigned herself to what they had to do. "All right, fine. Here's my Visa. Give us two rooms—one for me, and one for the gentleman." The man smirked at Jonas, clearly amused by that fact that Catherine did not want to share a suite with him. Undaunted, Jonas met the man's eyes and gave him a long, hard look.

"You heard the lady," he said evenly.

The clerk was the first to glance away. "Very good, sir," he said a bit more respectfully. He took Cat's card and began busily to pull out the necessary paperwork.

"You don't have to pay for me, Cat," Jonas told her.

"I know. And you didn't have to buy my ticket. So there."

He seemed to accept this as an answer and inclined his head graciously.

They waited while the desk clerk made the necessary arrangements and answered his questions as needed. To Catherine, it felt like an eternity before he handed the piece of plastic back to her along with floor plan for the hotel. "Miss, you are here . . ." He showed her on the map. ". . . and the gentleman is just down the hall here." He pointed out that room as well, then gestured in the direction they should go.

"Thank you." Catherine took the keys from his outstretched hand. "And now, you were saying something about the beach . . . ?"

The clerk drew one hand along his jaw line, making a great show of considering her words. "I have heard that there is a fine place for couples to go and walk together under the moon. I am afraid, however, that I cannot remember at the moment where that might be—"

"What do you mean?" What did he want now? Cat was about ready to jump out of her skin. They had come too far for her to be stopped by a game-playing desk clerk. She wanted to see Daphne *this instant*.

Jonas stepped forward and held out something which he slipped into the man's hand. "We appreciate your help.

Here's a little something for the effort."

"You're bribing him?" Catherine hissed.

"No," Jonas said innocently. "It's a tip."

"Fifty dollars isn't a tip. It's a dirty payoff," she complained.

Whatever it was, it seemed to work. "Thank you, sir!" Their friendly greeter perked right up. "May I suggest taking a walk upon our own private beach before you retire? If you go down that hallway"—he pointed—"turn right at the end of the hall, and exit through the French doors you see there, you will find yourselves on our back patio. From there, it is less than a hundred feet to the ocean's edge. I'm sure you will enjoy your walk out under the stars."

"Thanks," Jonas said dryly. "You've been a big help."

Catherine was already headed for the doors.

"Wait," Jonas called after her. "Don't you want to stash your things?"

"No," she said. "I want to find Daphne."

He shook his head and pointed to the purse and shoulder bag she had dumped in the corner. "Cat, you know I adore you. But I am not schlepping your carry-on bag all the way down a five-mile stretch of beach. If you don't want to put it in your room, you'll have to carry it yourself."

"Hmph." Cat glowered at him. "Chivalry is apparently dead."

"That's not fair. I'm chivalrous; I'm just not stupid."

She looked wounded. "I thought you *wanted* to carry my bags. You've been taking them from me all day."

"I have. But there's a limit even to *my* generosity."

"Okay, okay." She relented.

After a brief stop at their rooms, they retraced their steps and found their way out to the hotel's back patio. Catherine picked her way over the orange Spanish-style tiles that ended at the edge of a vast stretch of golden sand.

The mugginess of the evening was tempered by warm night winds. Cat drew in a deep breath of fresh sea air and listened to the soft lapping of the Caribbean waters against the shore.

"Which way do we go now?" Jonas asked.

"You've got me." Cat looked first to the north, then to the south, feeling torn. "I suppose we could each take a different direction."

"*Uhn*-uh." He looked horrified. "No way. Do you think I'm letting a beautiful woman like you wander around the grounds of a tropical resort *alone*? At *night*? I may be crazy, but I'm no fool."

His face was barely visible in the moonlight, which left dark shadows on its planes. Catherine longed to reach out and touch them but held her hands close to her sides. Jonas eyed her affectionately. "Nope, I'm sticking right by you, as long as you'll have me."

As long as that, Jonas? Catherine's heart cried out to him.

A mixture of emotions played across Jonas's strong features. She watched as uncertainty, longing, and hopefulness each made an appearance. Then, at last, desire won out, and he pulled her into the shelter of his embrace.

The crashing of the waves faded in the distance as Cat became aware only of the strong arms that closed around her. Without another word, Jonas lowered his face to hers. And in that next moment, Catherine found herself the recipient of a kiss far purer, far more passionate than the one she had once created in her dreams.

It lasted but a moment, but Cat knew she would never recover. Breathless, she drew back and smiled timidly up into the face she knew—and, yes, loved—so well.

"Cat," Jonas began raggedly. "I've tried not to push you.

But I can't hold back any longer; I *have* to tell you how I feel. I can't stop thinking about you, can't get you out of my mind. I thought maybe it was just an infatuation with a woman I once cared for, but it goes much deeper than that. I've been praying for guidance. And I think I have an answer. No, I *know* I have an answer."

He tightened his grip about her waist, drawing her even closer. "You see, it all comes down to this one thing. I've waited for years to find the right woman. And now it's clear. The only woman I could ever love is—"

"*Catherine?*" The word echoed in the summer night air.

Jonas blinked at Catherine. Catherine blinked back.

"Did you say that?" he said hopefully.

"Nope. You?"

"*Unh*-uh."

Realization dawned on them at exactly the same time.

Catherine practically jumped out of Jonas's embrace as she spun around to identify the source of the cry. Immediately she spotted a woman with hair just like Lucy's running toward them from the south end of the beach, a young, dark-haired man with a striking resemblance to Jonas following close behind.

"I can't believe it," Cat muttered to herself. She didn't know whether to leap for joy or cry out in pain. "I mean, Daphne's always had bad timing. But *this* is ridiculous."

Her youngest sister was nearly out of breath by the time she reached them. She clutched at Catherine's arms with both hands.

"Is it really you, Kitty? Thank God! Oh, I can't believe you're actually here!"

And with those unexpected words, she threw herself into Catherine's arms and collapsed into a fit of tears.

★ ★ ★ ★ ★

It was a full fifteen minutes—fifteen chaotic minutes filled with crying, angry outbursts, and accusations—before the group had calmed down enough for any sort of reasonable communication to take place.

Catherine, for her part, was certain that Elliott had done something to take advantage of her sister. "No, no! Get back!" she kept insisting, pushing away Elliott's hands as he reached across her to pat Daphne on the arm. "Don't you think you've done enough damage, Mr. I-Wanna-Run-Away-and-Elope?"

She sounded ridiculous and she knew it. But she didn't care. After three days of worrying, she finally had an opportunity to vent her frustrations on the man she now considered to be the cause of great pain to her—and, now it seemed, to her sister.

Elliott tried to explain, but Catherine would have none of it. Stepping in to defend his brother, Jonas added his own voice to the melee.

And Daphne, seemingly oblivious to the uproar she had caused, continued to sob while her sister comfortingly patted her back and stroked her soft crown of curls.

Finally, after several minutes, Daphne seemed to realize what was happening and opened her mouth to explain. But by this time, all parties were yelling at once. Finally, with both throats and ears hurting, the four decided to sit down and settle the matter like reasonable adults.

They made their way back to the patio and sat at a small grouping of chairs. It was then that Daphne finally was able to make Catherine understand that Elliott had not harmed her in any way.

"It's not what you're thinking," she said, drawing a deep breath and wiping her face on her sleeve. "Elliott has been a perfect gentleman."

"Then what's the matter? Did you have a fight?" Cat eyed Elliott suspiciously. As far as she was concerned, he was still the enemy. He averted his gaze to avoid her accusatory stare.

"No, it's not that," Daphne explained. "We were just down by the water, talking. We were going through all the details about tomorrow, and it's going to be beautiful and all, but . . ." Her face clouded over and she let out a whole new burst of tears. "But it's not what I wanted, Cat!" She hiccuped softly. "I'm sorry. I know I look like a basket case. It's just that this whole week has been so emotional. . . ."

Catherine stared at her dumbly. "What do you mean, it's not what you wanted? You've turned the world upside down to have this wedding, and to have it just this way."

"I know, I know," Daphne said miserably. "And it's almost perfect, really. But . . . I just wanted my family to be here, you know? You and Lucy and Fee. And my friends . . ." She turned to her fiancé, who sat in the chair beside her, and grabbed his hand for comfort. "I *want* to marry Elliott," she said with feeling. "But it just doesn't feel like I imagined it would."

Catherine's mind raced. This was exactly the opportunity she'd been hoping for. She couldn't have planned it better if she'd tried. Daphne was undecided; she was feeling weak. It wouldn't take much effort at this point for Cat to stop the wedding.

But as she looked into Daphne's eyes, Cat realized to her surprise that she no longer felt the desire to do so. All she wanted now was to help make things right for her baby sister. Wedding or no wedding, she wanted not what was sensible, but what was best. The only problem was, she didn't *know* what was best.

The realization that she wanted so badly to fix the situation reminded her of what she'd told Jonas during their walk on Catalina: *"I want God to make things right . . ."*

Suddenly she had her answer.

"Look," she said to Elliott, "I'm sorry I jumped all over you." It hurt to concede that she was wrong, but it was obvious this was the case. She had no other choice.

"It's all right. I understand." Elliott spoke plainly. "You were concerned for Daphne. I am too."

"Yes, but it was wrong of me." Catherine was impressed by the quiet dignity the young man demonstrated. Clearly he was in love with her sister; he also seemed mature enough to forgive quickly. Perhaps he would not be such a terrible brother-in-law, after all. "I hope you'll forgive me. I guess this is an emotional time for all of us," she remarked ruefully.

She turned to Jonas then, who sat watching her approvingly, to see if he would take charge. He seemed to feel no need, however, to direct the potential bride and groom. All three looked to her, clearly expecting . . . something. Daphne and Elliott appeared to be steeling themselves for a lecture. Jonas, in contrast, seemed perfectly at ease.

Catherine took a deep breath. She knew what she had to do.

"Obviously you two have a big decision to make," she began. "You care for each other very deeply, or you wouldn't be here at all. The feelings you've had for each other over the past few months count for a lot. But the feelings you're going through *tonight* count for a lot too. I don't think you should jump into anything. You must think about what you're doing very carefully."

Daphne hunched her shoulders and looked at Cat miserably. It was clear what she expected.

"But don't let the emotions of the moment dictate your decision either," Cat continued, ignoring the look of surprise this comment elicited. "Remember, it's—" She glanced at her watch. "My goodness, it's after one in the morning. Now is definitely *not* the time to make decisions that are going to affect the rest of your life. I suggest that you both go to sleep, get a good night's rest, and in the morning—when you feel better—you can talk again about whether or not to go ahead with your plans. What time is the wedding supposed to take place?"

"Eleven," Elliott said.

"Okay." She clapped her hands together. "Let's go back to our rooms then. Why don't you two meet for breakfast in the morning and talk about this some more? Jonas and I will come if you want us to." She gave her companion a knowing glance. "But if you want to be alone, that's perfectly okay too."

Daphne stared at her sister, as if she could not believe what she was hearing. Catherine pushed ahead. "And by the way, before you meet together, I think it would be a good idea for you to spend some time talking to God about what you should do."

She felt a bit hypocritical, suggesting that they do something she rarely did herself. But Jonas had made his point well, and she felt an inner urging to guide the two in that direction—as well as to spend some time on her knees herself.

"I know," she said. "I forget to pray about things too. But it's important. When you forget what matters most, it's too easy to let the things you value just slip away." The smile she gave Jonas was bittersweet. His eyes met hers and held them. "At least for a while."

Still confused, Daphne looked from him to her sister. "Is there something going on here I should know about? Because you two are acting like—"

Her mouth dropped open and she covered it with one small hand. "Oh! I forgot! When I came up, the two of you were—" She grabbed at Elliott's hand. "I was so wrapped up in what was happening with me, it didn't even register that they—" Even under the cover of nighttime, the reddening of her cheeks could be plainly seen. "I'm *sooo* embarrassed."

"No need to be," Jonas said cheerfully. He reached out, took her hand, and pulled his potential sister-in-law to her feet. "I'm sure Cat and I will pick up our . . . er, conversation at a future date." He stepped over to Catherine's side and whispered, "That's a promise."

Daphne needed no further urging to call it a night and was easily led back to the hotel lobby. After giving her sister a hug and a kiss, Cat turned to follow Jonas in the direction of their rooms. She had barely gone two steps when she felt a slight pressure on her arm.

She turned to find Daphne smiling at her.

"I was just wondering," Daphne said, "if you would . . ."

"Yes?" Catherine prompted.

"If you would come back to my room and pray with me?" Daphne looked as though she was afraid Cat might refuse.

Catherine felt a rush of gratitude. This, *this* was the type of relationship she had wanted with her sister for so many years. "Of course I will." She laughed self-consciously. "As long as I remember how."

"It's just like riding a bike," Jonas reassured her. "You never forget." He placed an arm around her shoulders and gave her a gentle squeeze. "You girls don't stay up too late now," he said affectionately. And then he was gone.

That night, Catherine spent a good twenty minutes in her sister's room, listening to Daphne's wide range of concerns and joining her in a short but heartfelt time of prayer. It was nearly two o'clock by the time the younger woman's weary head hit the pillow. But Cat left the room feeling confident that her sister had benefited from having someone to listen to her worries.

It was funny, Cat thought as she followed the carpeted hallway back to her own room. After all the time Cat had spent trying to control and protect Daphne, it had turned out to be her love and support, not her advice, that helped Daphne the most. This was particularly reassuring because, aside from reminding her to keep on praying, Catherine had little more advice to give. For once in her life, she had no idea what was the right thing to do. She knew that Daphne still had a lot of growing up to do. But maybe marriage was the crucible in which God intended for her to learn.

All logic pointed to waiting. And yet Catherine was beginning to understand that it was difficult to do so where love was concerned. She was beginning to understand that the pull of love is a very strong thing.

By eight o'clock on the morning of the wedding, the St. Lucia Resort was already bustling with activity. Outside the window of her second-story room, Catherine heard the delighted cries of children splashing in the hotel pool. From the next room came the faint hum of a hair dryer.

There was no need to leave her bed to experience the splendors of the tropics. From her cozy nest of blankets, Cat could see through an enormous window that looked out over the deep blue Caribbean. Within her own room, the unmistakable aroma of mangoes wafted from an arrangement of fruit ripening in a basket on her dresser. And somewhere in the distance, a bird unlike any she had ever heard before offered up a lilting, sunny melody.

Cat usually depended on her early-morning workout to help her become fully functional. But on her first day in St. Lucia she threw back the covers, immediately awake and alert—even after staying up into the wee hours of the night—and feeling thoroughly ready to explore the modern

Garden of Eden that beckoned outside.

A splash of cool water to the face and a quick once-over with her hairbrush were all Cat needed to become basically presentable. She threw on a simple white blouse, a papaya-colored wraparound skirt, and apricot espadrilles and headed for the door. Then, on impulse, she ran back to the bathroom to apply a touch of mascara and a dab of apricot lipstick. Jonas would be out there somewhere. "Basically presentable" did not seem nearly good enough.

Grabbing a mango from the basket, she stepped out the door, locked it behind her, and headed down to breakfast. After a couple of false starts, she found it being served on the patio where they had met the night before. In a corner near the sand she spotted a bleary-eyed Elliott talking intently with his older brother. Daphne was nowhere to be seen.

"Good morning, gentlemen." Cat plopped herself down beside them and took a juicy bite of mango. "Where's Daph?"

"I can't find her," Elliott said miserably. The night before, he'd seemed a confident, devoted fiancé. This morning, he looked troubled and overwhelmed . . . and young. He poked with his fork at a plate of cold scrambled eggs. "She's not in her room. I've looked all over."

Catherine frowned. "That's strange. How long has she been missing?"

"I knocked on her door at seven. That was . . ." He consulted his watch. ". . . almost an hour ago." He started to pop a bit of cold toast into his mouth. "It's not that I'm worried about *us*, Catherine. Daphne and me, I mean. I know she loves me. I just want to know that she's okay."

Cat thought for a moment. "She's not on the beach?"

"Not that I can see," he said. "She would have to have walked pretty far."

"I did."

The three of them spun around at the sound of Daphne's voice. Catherine's expression relaxed as she saw her sister offer up a timid smile. *Oh, thank goodness.* After all they'd been through, beginning a whole new search for Daphne was the last thing she wanted to do. Even more important, she—like Elliott—had been worried about the young woman's state of mind.

"Where were you?" Elliott asked her, scooting his chair over to make room for his bride. "I was worried."

Daphne settled in beside him and slipped her hand into his. "I've been awake since before six, going over all this in my mind," she confessed. "So I went for a long walk this morning to think about everything . . . about what I really want. I spent a little time talking with God too." Catherine could not help but reflect that the time had been good for her sister. Daphne looked more calm and composed than she had the night before. Come to think of it, after her own time in prayer the night before, she felt strangely peaceful herself.

"You know," Daphne said, looking at Cat curiously, "things feel very different to me here. Back home, all I wanted to do was get away from the family. I felt smothered . . . mis-understood." Cat, stung by a twinge of guilt, opened her mouth to reply but then closed it again, reminding herself to let her sister have her say.

"Elliott understands me though," Daphne said, eyeing him affectionately. "And he loves me. I know that. Being with him—well, I wanted more than anything to be his wife. I was in such a hurry to get married and then come home and begin our life together. . . ." For the first time, her confidence seemed to falter.

"It wasn't until I got here that I realized how scared I was." She looked at Elliott nervously. "Not of marrying *you*, but of what it would be like to *be* married. It felt good . . . but

218

too fast." His expression remained unreadable as Daphne squeezed his hand and implored him, "Elliott, please understand. I love you so much! I want to be your wife. But . . . ," she hesitated. "I'm pretty sure this isn't the right way to do it. Not for us." She looked then as if she might cry. "If I said I wanted to wait a little longer, would you hate me forever?"

Elliott sat quietly for a moment, then he raised his eyes to Daphne's and gave her a solemn wink. "I wouldn't hate you even for one second." Relief flooded over Catherine as she watched her sister throw her arms around him and shed the tears that had risen to her eyes. "Hey," he said soothingly, "You don't need to be afraid to tell me what you want or need. I *love* you, remember? I want what's best for you. For us."

Thank you, God, Catherine prayed silently. "You were right," she said, smiling at Jonas.

"I generally am," he grinned. "But what specifically am I right about this time?"

"Your brother really *is* a great guy."

Daphne leaned back, wiped her runny nose and pretended to glare at her sister. "Hey. I was right about that too."

"So you were," Catherine mused, watching as Elliott dabbed awkwardly at the tears on Daph's cheeks with a napkin, whispered in her ear, and somehow prompted a gentle laugh. "So you were."

She averted her eyes for a few moments and hummed to herself quietly as the two lovebirds whispered to each other about the decision they had just made. After a few minutes, the matter looked reasonably settled. Her tears spent, Daphne turned back to the others at the table.

"Well," she said, looking a bit sheepish. "So much for that. This feels a bit odd. What are we supposed to do now? It doesn't look like there's going to be a wedding after all."

"Not necessarily." Jonas grinned from ear to ear, looking

like the cat who swallowed the canary.

"*Jonas!*" Catherine hissed. She gave him a pointed stare. The decision was made. What was he doing, trying to talk Elliott and Daphne back into getting hitched? She shook her head and tried, unsuccessfully, to kick him underneath the table. There was no doubt about it. She was in love with a crazy man.

"What are you talking about?" Elliott looked puzzled. "We just told you we're going to wait."

"I know," Jonas said. He pushed his chair back from the table and considered each of their faces in turn. "I heard you. And I think you're making a wise decision. But . . ." His brow furrowed. "I can't help worrying about all those nonrefundable deposits you've made."

Elliott shrugged. "That's okay," he said, sounding unconcerned. "We'll get most of it back. It shouldn't be too big of a loss."

"That's true." Jonas scratched his stubbled chin thoughtfully. "Then, of course," he said after a moment, "there's the fact that you—and, of course, Catherine and I—flew all the way over here to the island paradise of St. Lucia for . . . what? Nothing really."

Daphne and Elliott stared at him. Jonas pushed himself up off the chair and began to pace around the area surrounding their table.

"And it hurts my heart," he said dramatically, clutching one hand to his chest, "to know that we've come to one of the most beautiful islands in the world—the most romantic place I've ever seen—and now there's going to be no wedding at all." He let his head drop so his chin rested heavily against his chest. "What a waste."

Catherine felt her cheeks grow red with anger. This was too much! Who did Jonas think he was, shaming those two poor kids for not having a wedding just because the decision had somehow messed up his plans? Well, she'd show him she had a thing or two to say about that! It didn't matter if she was in love with him or not. No one messed with her family. No one pushed them around. Not even Mr. Jonas Riley . . .

Jonas's head snapped back up. "Of course," he said, sounding cheerful again, "if we go ahead and have a wedding, that means we'll have to stick around here for another week."

Catherine stared at him in horror. How could she have so completely misjudged him? "*Now* what are you trying to talk these two into? Have you lost your mind completely?"

"But, my dear, sweet, Cat," he said in a voice like honey. "Have you forgotten what I told you on the plane? We would have to be in residence here two days before applying for a license. And then it's not good until another four days after that . . ."

"I'm sorry." Catherine tilted her head to one side and banged at one temple with the heel of her palm. "I thought for a moment there you said 'we' would have to be in residence—"

"Aha!" he cried happily. "*Now* you're catching on!" He stopped his pacing and came to her side. "These two have already decided that they prefer to wait. Who else would be in the market for a good wedding site except us?"

"I wasn't aware that we were in the market at all." Catherine tried to keep her face straight. But between Daphne's giggles and the singing of her heart, she was unable to prevent the joyous smile that rose to her lips.

"Silly woman," Jonas said fondly, then dropped to one knee. "Ouch!" he said as his kneecap hit the pavement.

"Are you okay?" Without thinking Catherine had stretched out her hand and touched his shoulder in a gesture of concern.

"Quite all right." He winced, then smiled and took her hand in his. She didn't draw it away.

"Good. You were saying . . . ?"

Jonas grinned at her then, the confident smile of a man who knew he had at last secured the affections of the woman he loved.

He held her hand tightly in his and pulled it against his heart. "Marry me, Cat? Say you will."

Cat's eyes twinkled.

" 'You will,' " she quipped.

Jonas eyed her sternly. "No, say *you* will."

She matched the seriousness of his expression and tone. " '*You* will.' "

He rolled his eyes heavenward. "Everyone's a comedian. Doesn't this woman ever take *anything* seriously?" Across the table from them, Elliott and Daphne joined in their laughter.

The sound warmed Catherine down to the depths of her soul. Just one week earlier, Daphne had warned her she was becoming old before her time. But now everything had changed.

"Come on, Cat," Jonas urged, impatience creeping into his voice. "I've waited twelve years. Tell me that you love me."

"Oh, I do," she said with feeling, not wanting to keep him waiting a moment longer. "I love you, Jonas. With all my heart."

His face flushed with pleasure. But he was not through.

"Tell me that you'll become my wife," he insisted.

"Sweetheart," Catherine said, reaching out to pull him up from his knees. In less than a second, they were both on their feet and in each other's arms. "Of course I'll marry you." As he lowered his face toward hers, she gave him a teasing smile.

"What took you so long? I thought you'd never ask."

"Why, you—" Jonas growled. But the scolding ended there, as he pulled her to him and sealed their promise with a fiercely soulful kiss.

For Catherine, the moment seemed frozen in time—as if it might last forever. Apparently the rest of their party felt the same way.

Daphne cleared her throat loudly.

"Hey!" Elliott protested. "Get control of yourselves, you two."

Cat pulled back slightly, and turned to her future brother-in-law with a grin.

"Actually Cat's never been this out of control in her life," Daphne observed.

Catherine looked at her curiously. "You know, I haven't." She never would have thought she'd find herself in this place—making a decision that felt so impulsive, and yet so right. Somehow, giving up control didn't seem so terrible anymore.

"That's okay, sweetheart," Jonas said gently, pulling her close once again. "You'll manage. In fact, this may be the beginning of a whole new life for you."

"Really?" Cat asked, snuggling close. But she felt certain he was right.

"Trust me," he said confidently.

And as she rested her cheek against the broad expanse of his chest, Catherine knew without a doubt that trusting Jonas was something she would be doing for a long, long time.

EPILOGUE

"You sleepy?"

Lazily Catherine opened one eye and glanced at the man sitting close to her on the boat's deck. "Nope," she lied.

"You could have fooled me. I was sure I'd heard snoring," Jonas said, playfully poking her in the foot with one big toe.

"Mmm. Must have been the motor." Cat did not stir.

"It certainly sounded like it, but the motor's off, love. We're sailing."

Obligingly she closed her eye again and faked the loudest, most obnoxious snore she could muster.

"That's it exactly," her husband said approvingly.

"It's the heat of the sun that's making me this way."

"Poor baby. But speaking of the sun: Come over here and I'll put more lotion on you."

"Oh, all right. If you must," Cat said with mock reluctance. She pushed herself to a sitting position and scooted closer beside him. "But I already feel like I'm about to slide off deck." In truth, she relished the thought of another gentle massage from her new husband's hands. She let out a wide yawn before submitting to Jonas's ministrations.

As soon as he began to work on her back, she felt herself relax even further—a feat she hadn't thought possible. "Ooh, you're good," she said with admiration. "Why does this feel so *wonderful?* I shouldn't be sore at all. In fact, you'd think all my muscles would have atrophied by now, we've been so lazy for the past couple of weeks."

"It's all that stress you've been hanging on to all these years," Jonas reasoned. "It's going to take a while for your body to release it. But I'll do all I can to help," he offered, gently running his fingers along the nape of her neck.

"How *generous* of you," Catherine laughed and turned to face him.

"Shh," Jonas hushed her, planting a soft kiss on her lips. He placed one hand on her shoulder and turned her to face front once again. "Just relax. Think of something that makes you happy."

"Mmm . . . if you insist." For once she was glad to do as she was told. The only difficult part was settling in on one specific memory, for the last few weeks had been the most glorious of her life.

On the day she accepted Jonas's proposal, she had found herself faced with countless decisions, including whether or not to get married on St. Lucia as Jonas suggested. After a morning of soul-searching, discussions with her fiancé, and heartfelt prayer—and with the approval of all three of her sisters—Cat had breathlessly chosen to take the plunge.

Fortunately Daphne and Elliott had already been through the process and were able to help her sort out all the details. Airline tickets were purchased for family members, a reasonable amount of food and flowers ordered, a minister selected, vows written, and a beach site chosen. By the end of her second day on St. Lucia, with nothing else to do but wait for the paperwork to come through, Cat had been ready to settle down and have some serious fun in the sun—which she did with the single-minded devotion she had, to this point, reserved for her career.

Not that she had walked away from work completely. She continued to check in with the office on a daily basis up until the day of the wedding. By then she had already learned that

Apollo Athletics, in the absence of Jonas and both Salinger sisters, had gone with a third competitor.

To her surprise, Cat could not bring herself to feel very sorry about losing the account. Although there had been a fair amount of money and prestige at stake, the impromptu campaign was one that neither she nor Daphne was proud of. She did harbor some guilt on Jonas's account—after all, he, too, had lost the business, and all because of her. But Jonas showed no signs of regret. "We're in this together," he reminded her. "Besides, I won a much better prize—you."

Cat wasn't about to argue. Nor was she about to let the joy of the moment slip away. Willingly she had agreed to relinquish her control of the company for the next few weeks. It wasn't as difficult as she had thought it would be. From the sound of things, Davis Pierce and Carol Kincaid had things under control at the office, although Davis was a bit pouty about her sudden elopement. Cat's concern over this, however, was brief—lasting only until Carol informed her that Davis had already taken out Carol's eldest daughter, Lisa, and was furiously working on sweet-talking her into a second date.

He'll survive, Catherine told herself. *So will Salinger & Associates. Let it go, Cat. Just follow your heart.*

And so, just one week after her arrival in St. Lucia, she had found herself standing at the edge of the glorious Caribbean, pledging her life to the man of her dreams.

Jonas leaned forward, interrupting her reverie. "Whatcha thinking about?" His sweet breath tickled her ear.

"Our wedding day." Cat sighed with contentment. "Didn't we just have the best one ever?"

"We did," he agreed confidently.

"My only regret," she said with a touch of sadness, "is that Robin couldn't be there."

"That would have been a neat trick," Jonas laughed. "Considering that she was in labor at the time."

Catherine made a face. "I'm glad I didn't know about it until afterward. I would have been a basket case!" She turned to face him. "Thank you," she said soberly, "for flying me home to see her and baby Annie the next day."

Jonas threw up his hands in a gesture of defeat. "Hey, I knew the score. If you hadn't seen that baby, and *pronto,* I never would have gotten you to enjoy a proper honeymoon. Besides, it worked out for the best, don't you think? We'd already explored the Caribbean. This way, we got to see the Pacific a bit—and revisit the place where you fell in love with me again after all these years." He grinned wickedly.

Cat rolled her yes. "Pretty sure of yourself, aren't you, mister?"

"What I am sure of, my love," he said fondly, "is you."

At just that moment, their gruff little captain poked his head above deck.

"You lovebirds thought much about where yer headed next?"

"You'd better believe it," Jonas told him without hesitation. He reached out, and Catherine willingly settled into the strong shelter of his embrace. "Straight into the future . . ."

"You heard him, Big Jack." Cat wrapped her arms tightly around Jonas's neck, her eyes filled with tears of joy. "And right into the best years of our lives."